THE PMS CLUB

Other books by Carolyn Brown:

Trouble in Paradise
The Wager
Love Is
A Falling Star
All the Way from Texas
The Yard Rose
The Ivy Tree
Lily's White Lace
That Way Again

The *Love's Valley Historical Romance* Series:

Redemption
Choices
Absolution
Chances

The *Promised Land Romance* Series:

Willow
Velvet
Gypsy
Garnet
Augusta

The *Land Rush Romance* Series:

Emma's Folly
Violet's Wish
Maggie's Mistake
Just Grace

THE PMS CLUB

•

Carolyn Brown

Montlake
Romance

Published by Montlake Romance
P.O. Box 400818
Las Vegas, NV 89140

ISBN-13: 9781477813058
ISBN-10: 1477813055

To Kenneta and Lola Rice

Chapter One

"You're not about to go gallivantin' down there all summer. Good lord, Dixie, what can you be thinkin' about? What would people say? Everyone in town is already hearin' weddin' bells and they're chimin' just for us," Todd said lazily, combing his thick blond hair back with his fingertips.

"Well, I don't remember you proposing, Todd Riley. I can't remember a moonlight dinner in a fancy café over in Little Rock or a diamond ring or anything like that. Maybe my memory is fading like my youth," Dixie said from across the massive dining room table.

"Didn't think I had to do all that folderol. Just figured we'd go get a plain gold band on the way to the courthouse. Good lord, Dixie, you know how I feel about you. I just reckoned we'd get married about August and you could quit your job and start havin'

1

babies and be happy. By the way, the first one should be a boy. Todd Riley the fifth to make Momma and Daddy happy," Todd said.

"You just reckoned! You just reckoned!" she repeated, unable to believe what he'd said.

"You are not going and that's the end of the conversation," Todd pushed his coffee cup across the table toward her. "Mind gettin' me a refill?"

"Get your own coffee, and that's not the end of this conversation," Dixie stood up and leaned across the table, her nose just inches from Todd's, her green eyes glistening. "Where do you get off telling me what I can and can't do? I'm thirty-five years old. I *reckon* I can make my own decisions."

"Sure you can, honey. You can decide to marry me and have my children. You can decide to stay home and raise them proper like my momma did. That's what you can decide," he said icily.

"And now Sara Evans with her new number one single, and I don't even have to tell you the title," the radio DJ said and the song began about a young girl leaving so quick that she left the suds in the bucket and the clothes hanging out on the line.

"That's what you want, isn't it?" Dixie said. "A sweet little wife who'll stay home and do the laundry out on the back porch in a washtub."

"Not literally," Todd raised his coffee cup to remind her he wanted a refill. "But figuratively, yes, that's what I want—a woman who knows her place. Who stays home and makes a home for her family. Who fills up her husband's coffee cup when it's empty. Dixie, you know there's enough Riley money that I'd never spend all my inheritance in a lifetime. You don't have to work, honey, so what's this fight all about anyway? Besides, if you listen to that song, she's leaving her home to run away with the love of her life."

"Well, bless her heart. She may be leaving for a life with her true love. The difference in her story and mine is that I'm just leaving. I hope you find someone to keep that cup full and the clothes on the line, Todd," Dixie slapped the tabletop so hard that the crystal candlesticks rattled together. She picked up her purse and started out of the room, through the foyer and toward the front door.

"If you walk out that door, Dixie Nelson, it's over," Todd said. "No wedding. No children. You'll dry up an old maid."

Dixie didn't even look back.

She drove three miles back into the town of Greenbrier, parked her car in the garage and locked the door. She went through the two-bedroom house mentally checking off each task. Thermostat was turned off. No need to cool a house all summer when she wouldn't be there. Timer set on the lamps in the living room to come on at different times throughout the three months she'd be gone.

By the time she heard the honk in the driveway, all she had to do was pick up her bags, turn on the security alarm and lock the door. Jill and Faith waved to her from the Jeep Cherokee and motioned that she was to load her things into the back.

"So how did it go with Todd? He going to come see

you every weekend? Somehow I can't see him walking in the sand in his bare feet," Faith grinned.

"We won't be seeing Todd," Dixie said.

"No!" Jill drove with one hand and covered her mouth with the other in one of her famous dramatic gestures. "You didn't break up with Todd. Everyone in town says you'll probably be married before the new year."

"Guess everyone in town is wrong. We did break up. He's living in the wrong age. It's probably his parents' fault," Dixie said.

"They didn't potty train him right?" Faith asked in mock seriousness.

"No, it's all that money," Dixie told her two best friends. "They think because they're rich they can sit on their thrones and play God. The whole bunch of them would have been better off if they'd been born about thirty years before the Civil War."

"What'd you fight about?" Jill drove south toward Interstate 40. They'd take that route to Memphis, Tennessee, then head south to Florida. By bedtime they'd be at the beach house.

"His crazy notions. He thought we'd just get married at the end of the summer. I'd quit my job and have babies and keep his coffee cup full," Dixie said.

"He proposed?" Faith asked.

"No, he demanded," Dixie said. "And I'm not quitting my job. I love teaching. And I'm not going to be his little live-in wifey person who jumps when he yells. I have opinions and ideas, too."

"What about that biological clock? It's been ticking

loudly for the past few months," Jill asked, looking in the rearview mirror to make sure Dixie wasn't crying.

"I just took the battery out of the damn thing for the next three months." Dixie grinned at Jill's worried reflection in the mirror. "Now enough about Todd Riley. Let's go have a wonderful summer."

"Look out men, here come three thirty-five-year-old women who can't hear a single ticktock," Jill said.

They'd been best friends five years, since the first day they'd come to the Greenbrier school system. They were the new ones that year. Jill, a widow of only a year, from Tulsa, Oklahoma, had made a move away from painful memories. Faith had come from New Orleans to Arkansas, escaping an ex-boyfriend's face everywhere she turned. Dixie had been born in Conway, just nine miles away, and brought up in Greenbrier. She'd taught in Conway where she earned her teaching degree until five years ago, when Greenbrier offered her a high school English position. Jill taught third grade. Faith taught junior high math.

The beach house they planned to live in all summer belonged to Faith's uncle. He'd offered it to Faith and her friends with only one small favor included. There were several big charity events during the summer in New Orleans. He'd told Faith that if she or either of her friends would accompany him to those affairs, they could have the beach house for the whole summer. Of course, Faith had accepted. She loved dressing up and seldom had the opportunity to in Greenbrier, Arkansas.

Dixie figured Faith Galaway had been the belle of the ball more times than she could count when she had lived in New Orleans. A tall, well-built blond with big round blue eyes and one of those true southern peaches-and-cream complexions. Sometimes a bit on the strange side when she started talking about putting curses on people with gris-gris bags, or reincarnation, or burning candles of different colors. Or even the matching periapts—amulets from Tibet—that they all wore. Weird in a funny way that kept Jill and Dixie both from being too grounded in reality and put a little mysterious spice into their lives.

Jill was the exact opposite. Grounded firmly in old traditional beliefs. Six years a widow, yet still hanging on to the memory of the good times she'd shared with her husband. A short brunette with brown eyes and an angular face, full wide mouth and heavy eyebrows that she had to constantly keep waxed or else she'd look like Groucho Marx.

Dixie had mentioned two weeks before that she and her friends were going away for the summer, but Todd had just laughed it off, saying that she couldn't live three whole months without him. She'd told him a week ago she'd made up her mind to go, but he'd casually changed the subject to some family reunion the Rileys were having at the original family mansion in Little Rock.

She'd gone to his house that morning to say good-bye and to make him finally understand that she wouldn't be home for three months. After that fiasco, she might not be home ever again. She just might stay in Florida forever.

"Want to talk about it some more?" Jill asked from the front seat.

"No, but I am hungry," Dixie said.

"Then you're still mad. Some women pout when they're angry. Some weep until their eyes are swollen. Dixie eats her way out of the rage," Faith said. "But now that you mentioned food, I'm hungry too. Cracker Barrel sound good? I'd go for some grits and eggs with a side order of pancakes and sausage."

"And maybe some hash browns and biscuits with blackberry jelly and an apple dumpling for dessert," Dixie said.

"Whew, she's talking apple dumplings, Jill. We'd better get her to the beach in a hurry. Think you can drive this Jeep any faster," Faith teased.

"It's six hundred and fifty miles. I'll have us there for a late-night swim before bedtime. Until then we'll just have to keep her fed and hope it does the job until the warm sand can work its wonders on her," Jill pulled into the Cracker Barrel Restaurant and nosed the Jeep into a parking spot close to the door.

"There ain't enough sand in the world to cool off my temper right now," Dixie said on the way into the restaurant.

"The English teacher just said 'ain't,' Faith. The anger is eating up her good sense. They'd better bring on the food fast," Jill grinned.

"Okay, talk, girl," Faith said when they'd been seated and given their orders to the waitress.

"A whole year I've been with Todd Riley, just hanging on his every word, waiting for him to propose. Known him all my life. Worried about him when his wife was killed in that house fire all those years ago. Never thought he'd ever pay any attention to me, though. I mean he was Todd Riley," she drew out all three syllables of his name with flicks of her wrist. "Now I find out he's nothing more than a male chauvinist wallowing in more gold than Fort Knox has."

"I've been telling you not to waste your time," Faith said. "He's so much like my ex-boyfriend it reeks."

"I know. I know," Dixie almost whined. "But he's so pretty and he kisses so good and I didn't want to believe you."

The waitress set a platter of biscuits before them and Dixie transferred two over to her saucer, lavishly buttering both of them, then adding a thick layer of blackberry jam.

"It's pure sin," Jill sipped black coffee. "If I ate like you do, I'd weigh two hundred pounds."

"Oh, you would not," Dixie said. "Besides, I told you before. Mad is an energy consuming thing. Nothing you eat when you're angry has fat grams or calories. It all goes to feed the rage."

"Then shoot the woman," Faith said in a wicked whisper. "If she's feeding it, it won't ever go away."

"No, you feed it until it becomes docile and tamable," Dixie polished off one biscuit and started on the other, motioning toward the waitress to bring them more.

"If I ate like that every time I got upset, I'd look like Mama Cass," Jill said.

"If I didn't, I'd be in jail for homicide," Dixie told them. "I think his exact words were, 'I just reckoned we'd get married about August and you could quit your job and start havin' babies and be happy.'"

"That's the way he proposed?" Faith almost choked on a bite of biscuit.

"That's it. No 'Darlin' I love you and can't live without you for three months.' Not even a sweet 'Please say you'll not see anyone while you're gone and you'll marry me when you get home.' Of course the prelude was 'You're not about to go gallivantin' down there all summer. Good lord, Dixie, what can you be thinkin' about? What would people say?' And the benediction was that if I walked out the door there'd be no wedding or children." She did a deep voice impersonation of Todd's southern drawl that was right on key.

"He's a true horse's butt," Faith said.

"A bonafide redneck Arkansas horse's butt, even if he is too rich to be a redneck," Jill nodded.

"Well, that's the story girlfriends, and I guess that leaves all three of us free, over twenty-one, and single for the summer," Dixie told them.

"No tears? You've been seeing him a whole year," Jill reminded her.

"No tears, and that darlin' is a promise," Dixie said. "If I get maudlin then remind me of what a romantic proposal I just got."

"Ticktock, ticktock," Faith jiggled her head from side to side.

"I took the battery out remember?" Dixie told her. "Besides, I forgot to tell you the best part. If I walked out the door there would be no marriage. No children. And, the very, very best part, I'd dry up an old maid. So dear hearts, I'm not putting the battery back until school starts on August 15."

Faith made the sign of the cross over her chest and dropped her head. "Forgive me, Father, for I am about to sin. I intend to burn black candles and say ancient chants over his sorry soul. He said those words to you? Old maid?"

"Dried up old maid," Dixie reminded her.

"He's in big trouble now," Jill giggled.

"Oh, yeah," Faith set her mouth in a firm line.

"The best thing we can do is ignore him. If he calls—and he does have the phone number because I gave it to him two weeks ago—tell him I'm gone. If I answer I'll hang up. It all sounds childish, but I don't even want to talk to him or about him anymore. Let's not spoil a perfect summer."

"To the perfect summer," Faith raised her coffee cup.

Chapter Two

Cool night breezes flowed gently down the beach.
The water lapped up to tickle Dixie's bare feet and then
retreated back. Stars decorated the sky like tiny
Christmas lights. The moon hung mystically amongst
the stars, a big round white ball that was supposed to be
viewed in the arms of a handsome man. With
Greenbrier, Arkansas, almost seven hundred miles
away, Dixie let go of her anger and replaced it with the
peace surrounding her, glad that Todd Riley wasn't
there to share the moon and stars with her. She might
have drowned the sorry son-of-a-gun and let the fish
have him for supper.

"Let's go watch *Steel Magnolias* and fall asleep in
front of the television with a bowl of popcorn," Jill
said.

"Sounds good to me. Be warned though, I won't get

11

to the part where Ouisa chops the tail end off that armadillo cake before I'm asleep. I'm not even hungry anymore," Dixie said.

"Good lord, she's over the mad spell. I told you if we got her to the warm sand and the ocean it would work miracles on her. You two go on and watch the movie again. I'm going to sit here a spell. I'd forgotten how much I miss the beach. Been five years since I've been back," Faith said.

"I can see why you'd miss it," Dixie said.

"Don't get a moonburn sitting out here. We'll watch the Ya-Ya's tomorrow night and get our PMS club all in order for the summer," Jill dusted off the back of her jean shorts and started up the stairs toward the three-bedroom house on the slight cliff above the beach.

"If I'm not at the house when the movie is over, come and wake me up," Faith yawned and threw herself back in the warm sand.

"Will do. And remember, Faith, our one rule for the summer," Dixie followed Jill up the stairs.

"We can only bring home one thing from the beach and it has to be approved by all three of us," Faith intoned. "Who made up that silly rule anyway?"

"You did," Jill and Dixie said in unison.

They microwaved popcorn, set a square box of tissues on the coffee table and put *Steel Magnolias* in the DVD player. Five years before they'd watched the movie together for the first time. Jill had invited them over for sandwiches and a movie and their friendship began over *Steel Magnolias*. It was also the beginning of the Sisterhood.

"Which spirit are you most like?" Faith had asked that night. "I'm Clairee."

"She's old," Dixie had protested.

"Spirit, I said, not body. I'm Clairee because she talks southern and she's rich as Midas and she doesn't care what people think of her," Faith had said.

"I'm Truvy," Dixie'd said.

"You're not married," Jill had argued.

"No, but I've never been anywhere but right here. Truvy is my spirit," Dixie declared.

"Then I'm Annelle," Jill had said. "Husband problems sent her packing. Not exactly the same as my situation but the same spirit."

"We're the Magnolias of Greenbrier, Arkansas," Faith had declared.

A couple of years later they watched *The Divine Secrets of the Ya-Ya Sisterhood* and instantly created their own Magnolia Sisterhood. Then one evening Faith had declared that they would be the Periapt Magnolia Sisterhood or, the PMS Club, and had presented Jill and Dixie with periapts to match the one she wore constantly. Small filigree silver circles worn on a silver chain. The periapts, she'd told them would protect them from mischief and disease. The amulets were Tibetan and became the official sign of the PMS Club, which would forever more have only three members.

They'd toasted with a bottle of cheap wine Jill had in the cabinet and the Periapt Magnolia Sisterhood Club was formed. Five years later after wars and rumors of wars, true PMS, men problems, school problems, through rich and poor, sickness and health, the PMS

Club still met every Monday night at Jill's house for sandwiches, a movie, and a general gritch-fest. Once a year they watched *Steel Magnolias* and the Ya-Ya's, used up a whole box of tissues, and swore they'd never watch either again.

M'Lynn was delivering her speech near the end of the movie about how she could run a mile but Shelby couldn't and how she'd brought that precious life into the world and she'd watched her leave the world. Jill and Dixie were wiping their eyes when Faith came bounding in the door.

"I found something on the beach and I want to keep it," she said, sitting down between them on the sofa and keeping the tissues handed out until the end credits rolled.

"What kind of seashell did you find? And are you sure you want to pick your one thing on the first night?" Dixie blew her nose loudly one more time and tossed the tissue into the wastepaper basket beside the sofa.

"It's of the male gender. It's about six feet tall and has the most gorgeous blond hair. It lives next door for the summer. It's going to be there all summer and I want to keep it. Lord, it's beautiful and young," Faith rolled her eyes dramatically.

"I don't think the periapt worked. You got into mischief," Dixie said.

"I ignored it, and he kisses good, too," Faith said.

"On the first date?" Jill said in mock horror.

"It wasn't a date so it didn't matter," Faith said.

"How young?" Dixie remembered what she'd said earlier.

"Twenty-six," Faith grimaced.

"Good lord, girl. He was in the second grade when you graduated high school. He could be one of your first year students," Jill did the calculations in her head. "You've been kissing a second grader? I think that's against the law."

"He's not a second grader now, honey, believe me. And we're going to walk on the beach at dawn. His name is Jackson by the way," Faith grinned mischievously.

"Not Jackson like Shelby's husband in the movie," Jill gasped.

"Yes, just like that. Only he's even prettier. And don't look at me like that. I'm not going to marry him and die," Faith said.

"Jackson what? And why is he here in Florida for the summer? And what else did you find out other than he kisses good and he's only twenty-six? He could be a serial killer or married," Dixie eyed her friend closely.

"Sure he could but he's not and he's really twenty-six and I didn't tell him how old I am so neither of you are going to either. Understood?" Faith cocked her head to the side like she did when she was very serious.

"Sure, we'll be real good and not tell. And we won't let him watch R-rated movies without your permission or give him cookies before dinner, either," Dixie teased.

"I'm going to bed. I have to be up before the crack of dawn," Faith pointed her finger at Dixie. "That's all you're allowed to tease me about Jackson. By the way, his last name is Smith and he doesn't wear either a wedding band or have a white line on his finger where one used to be."

"Good luck, Faith," Jill waved as she made her way across the floor to her own room. "And we'll wait to see how things work out before we vote on whether you get to keep him or not. If he's a good boy and doesn't pick his nose or whine, we'll think about it."

"That's your one allowable joke," Faith shook her finger at Jill. "If I'm not around when you two go to the store tomorrow, I want lots of juice, fruit, and yogurt. Uncle Vincent has a smoothie machine."

When Dixie awoke the next morning, the sun was high in the sky. Faith was gone. Jill had a bottle of sunscreen and a towel and was on her way out the back door.

"Hey, I thought we were going to the store," Dixie said, wiping sleep from her eyes.

"I left a list and some money on the counter. Faith put her list and money beside mine. The car keys are hanging on the hook beside the front door. Have fun and don't get into trouble," Jill waved on her way out.

"Well, blast it all," Dixie slapped the bar. She opened the refrigerator door. An apple, withered up like an ancient old woman's face. A quart of milk dated sometime last year. Two clear plastic storage bowls with the beginnings of either a terrible batch of guacamole or a fantastic penicillin culture, probably about enough to cure a national epidemic of summer colds.

With a grumbling stomach, she threw off her worn nightshirt and donned a pair of wrinkled khaki shorts and a T-shirt, slipped her feet into a pair of sandals and grabbed the car keys. They'd learn better than to send her to the store when she was hungry. She'd even buy brussels sprouts when her stomach was growling and they all three hated brussels sprouts.

She stopped at the first big market she found on the main strip and was on her way inside when she noticed a snow cone stand not far from the door. She bought a large rainbow without even thinking of calories. Creamy coconut, pineapple, and banana. Not so very colorful but it tasted like heaven, and kept her from going bankrupt in the grocery store.

Driving slowly and trying to take everything in at once on her way back to the beach house, she passed miniature golf courses, go-cart tracks, everything to keep a tourist busy twenty-four hours a day. She was glad she didn't have to condense her vacation down to a few days but could enjoy the whole summer in Florida. A T-shirt shop took her attention and had a parking place in front of it, a miracle within itself at that time of day. She parked and hopped out of the Jeep. She'd only stay a minute since she had perishables in the backseat, but a shirt hanging in plain sight with the ocean dry brushed on the front captured her attention.

She picked it up. The price wasn't absolutely exorbitant. It was a man's size extra large and would swallow her, but it would make a wonderful cover-up for her bikini. She planned on wearing it so much that by summer's end it would be faded, stained, and holey. She meandered through the small store. Little more than a shack really with a window propped up on a narrow bar that served as a checkout station. She held two other shirts, trying to decide whether to purchase them for

Jill and Faith when a shrieking noise made her practically jump out of her skin. By the time she'd uncovered her ears, she realized it was the burglar alarm on Jill's Jeep sounding like a cornered banshee. She ran outside to see who was trying to jimmy the lock and steal her friend's vehicle, only to have herself jerked around by the arm so quick that for a moment she didn't know if she was going outside the shop or back inside it.

"Lady, don't use someone's car alarm as an excuse to be stealing from me," a man said in a slow drawl.

"I'm not," she protested, looking up into the most handsome face she'd ever seen. Sunbleached blond hair, just a bit too long, feathered back perfectly. Light brown eyes with electric yellow highlights. Muscles, both on his chest and upper arms, stretching a T-shirt with a mermaid painted on the front.

"Oh, sure. You've got three shirts in your hands and I'm just so sure that Jeep is yours and you are running out there to see about it," he said.

"It is my car, or rather my friend's, and I'm using it today to buy groceries, and I am not stealing from you and if you'll let me go I'll stop that screeching before it deafens us all," she threw the shirts at him and pulled out of his grip, flustered, blushing crimson and muttering things under her breath unfit for human ears. She'd have a bruise on her arm tomorrow for sure. Maybe she should call the police and bring brutality charges against him.

He folded his arms across his chest and scowled at her while she fumbled in her purse and pushed the right buttons on the keychain to stop the noise. She did look like a tourist in those wrinkled shorts, faded T-shirt and her hair pulled back in a ponytail. All that creamy white skin meant she'd only just arrived in Pensacola. That and the brown bags of food showing in the back window of the Jeep. Maybe he'd been wrong, but it sure looked like she was running out of his store with three T-shirts that had taken him a couple of hours to paint.

"There now," Dixie told him. "I wasn't trying to steal from you and I do want the shirt with the beach scene on it, but you can rest assured I won't be coming back to do any more business with you."

"My apologies," he said through clenched teeth.

He laid the shirt on the counter and rang up the sale on an old fashioned cash register. One that had rows and rows of numbers. Dixie hadn't seen one like that since she was a child. More recently the grocery store in Greenbrier had installed those scan registers. She'd always missed the jangle of a price appearing in the window when the keys were pushed and the lever pulled.

"That will be twenty-four dollars and ninety-five cents," he folded the shirt and slipped it down into a plastic bag bearing the store logo.

"Is it true you are hiring?" Dixie nodded toward the small "Help Wanted" sign propped up beside the cash register and handed him a twenty and a five.

"Yes, it is. Need someone on Friday, Saturday, and Sunday mornings. Nine in the morning until three in the afternoon. Eighteen hours. Minimum wage. I can handle it alone except then," he put a nickel in her palm.

"I'd like to apply for that job. Do you have an application form?" she asked.

"You'd like to what?" He couldn't believe his ears.

"I'm living out on the beach, not a half a mile from here for the summer. I'll be bored out of my mind if all I do is burn and peel all summer. I think I'd like a part-time job. I'm Dixie Nelson. I'm from Greenbrier, Arkansas, and I'll be here until August 15, when I have to go back home for the school year. I'm a high school English teacher. I assure you I am not a shoplifter," she extended her hand toward him.

"I'm Boone Callahan. I'm only here for the summer months. I teach History in a junior college near San Antonio, Texas. Folks brought me here for a vacation when I graduated from high school and I fell in love with the place. Come here soon as classes are finished and spend my summers painting T-shirts. And you are hired if you're serious," he said.

"I'm serious as midterm grades," she smiled. "But I've got to admit, I am not artistic so if this job involves painting on shirts, you'd better reconsider."

"No, I'm the artist," he grinned. "I need someone to run the register, wait on customers, that kind of thing. I'll paint. You sell."

"I can do that," she said. "So do I begin day after tomorrow? I think that's Friday."

"Yes, you do, Dixie Nelson. Be here at nine," he said.

"Do I need to fill out forms?" She asked.

"I'll pay you contract labor. Every Sunday when you get ready to leave. That way neither of us has to do so much Uncle Sam work," he said. "That all right with you?"

"Sure," she said. "Then I'll see you Friday morning at nine, Boone Callahan."

She drove home with a big smile on her face. So her periapt hadn't worked so well either. She'd gotten into her own fair share of mischief that morning.

"Food!" Faith yelled from the doorway of the house and ran out to help unload groceries. "What are you grinning about? Did Todd call and offer to buy you half of Arkansas if you'd come back home to him?"

"No, he did not. I got a job," Dixie said.

"You did what?" Faith almost dropped the bag.

"I got a job at a T-shirt shop. Friday, Saturday, and Sunday from nine a.m. to three in the afternoon." Dixie set two bags on the counter.

"You did what?" Jill opened the back door.

"Oh, come on in and I'll tell you both. My periapt didn't work either. I was looking at this T-shirt," she pulled it from the sack and showed it to them. "Someone must have touched the Jeep because the alarm went off and I rushed out to see about it. The owner of the store thought I was trying to steal his shirts and he grabbed me. Anyway, by the time it was all settled I noticed he had this sign beside the cash register and I applied right there for the job and he hired me. And Faith, if you can keep what you found on the beach, then I want to keep Boone Callahan."

"Boone! Boone! As in Daniel?" Faith giggled. "I'd say that both our periapts have failed us. Is he twenty-six? Does he kiss good?"

"Didn't you hear me? He thought I was a shoplifter.

He sure wasn't interested in kissing me. And I don't know if it's Boone as in Daniel or what. Just that he teaches at a ju-co over around San Antonio, Texas, and spends his summers here painting T-shirts. But he is so handsome. Light brown eyes. Sun bleached blond hair. Muscles everywhere you look. If you take home your boy toy, can I keep him?" she teased.

"How old is he?" Jill asked, narrowing her eyes.

"I'd say about my age. I didn't ask," Dixie unloaded three one-quart containers of plain yogurt and two packages of strawberries into the refrigerator. The wrinkled apple didn't look quite as lonesome now.

"I'm jealous as hell," Jill kicked the trash can and pouted. "My periapt is working fine. I want it to fail so I can get into some mischief. It's not fair."

"It might not be working this weekend," Faith said.

"Oh?" Jill asked. "Does the day care center where you got Jackson have any more eligible bachelors?"

"I said you couldn't tease me anymore and I found out that the reason Jackson can take off a whole summer is because he's self-employed. He does something with computers and making those god-awful games the teenagers live and die for these days," Faith giggled. "Now, back to the failure of your periapt, Jill. Uncle Vincent has decided to give a bunch of money to a charity in Mobile. You are going in my place. He's sending a car Friday night. Jackson and I are clam digging and having a private party on the beach."

"Oh, no I'm not. I didn't bring anything to wear to something like that," she said.

"You got tomorrow to shop, honey. And it's very formal so buy something low-cut, sequined, and expensive. Keep the ticket. Uncle Vincent will pay for it. When he called a few minutes ago, he said he'd send the limo and that he'd give you an envelope with fifty thousand dollars in it. It's a bachelor auction. You bid on the bachelor of your choice and then he eats supper with you. Uncle Vincent is overweight and balding but he's delightful and he is the bachelor of your choice. You'll enjoy the evening and honey, you can kick any bunch of sea oats from here to New Orleans and all the rich bachelors will be running out to go to that auction so you can take your pick of the crop. It fluffs up their little egos to see how much the rich women will bid to eat with them. Uncle Vincent says you are his mystery lady that night. No one knows you. Oh, and he says you have to bid thirty thousand dollars on him even if the bidding looks like it's going to stop at fifty dollars. If you have money left in the envelope then you can bid on another bachelor and have dinner with two or three men. He intended to give the money to charity anyway and this is a fun way to do it."

"I'm not going," Jill said.

"Yes, you are," Dixie told her. "We'll shop this afternoon and tomorrow. Maybe you'll find something you want to keep other than a sequined dress cut down to here," she said and drew a line from between her breasts to her belly button.

"And what are the odds that the periapt won't work three times in less than a week?" Jill asked.

"I think it only works in Arkansas," Faith said. "But just to be safe, I said a chant over them while I was at the beach last night. When Jackson came walking by in the moonlight, I took their power from them for the rest of the summer."

"Then I get to keep Boone?" Dixie laughed.

"We'll have to see if he's keepable," Faith joined in the laughter. "At least you're not mad at Todd and hungry."

"Todd who?" Dixie asked all innocent-eyed.

Chapter Three

"Where on earth do we start?" Jill moaned when Dixie reached for the car keys beside the front door. "I don't have any idea what to wear to an affair like this. It's been years since I've socialized."

"Oh, come on Jill. Think of it as a PMS Monday night. Only with fancy clothes instead of sweats and sneakers, and some kind of food I can't even pronounce rather than bologna and cheese sandwiches. Of course you will have rich men to flirt with instead of two old tired teachers who've got a list of gripes to air. Now that might be the only reason to stay at home. The company won't be nearly as good," Dixie drove into town.

Jill couldn't suppress the giggle. Leave it to Dixie to give her a visual of tuxedo clad men eating bologna and whining about their lifestyles. "Well, tell me Miss

I-Have-All-the-Answers, where we go to find a dress like that. Oh, good lord, I'll need shoes too."

"Then we'll find shoes. And I know just where to start this journey for the perfect rich bachelor-finding dress," Dixie parallel parked right in front of the Ocean View T-shirt place.

"You've got to be kidding," Jill rolled her eyes in bewilderment.

"No, I figured with your looks you could wear a T-shirt with the image of Elvis on the front and get away with it at the benefit. Maybe tie up the side so your long legs will show. You will shave them, won't you? Don't want to give the folks down here the idea that we don't know how to dress and groom ourselves in Arkansas," Dixie said.

"I think I'm going to hyperventilate," Jill said.

"This is where my new job starts tomorrow morning. Boone has been here for years every summer. I betcha he can tell us where the exclusive little shops are," Dixie bailed out of the Jeep and motioned for Jill to follow her.

"Is this Friday?" Boone looked up from the cash register, a grin spreading across his handsome face. He'd wondered if Dixie would even come back, but no one else had applied for the job so he'd kept hoping she would.

"No, it's Thursday. Boone, this is my friend, Jill. She's got to go to a really fancy benefit auction tomorrow night over in Mobile. We need to find her a dress to wear to it and we only have today to find it," Dixie said.

"Right glad to make your acquaintance, ma'am," Boone extended his hand.

Jill smiled. A blind woman could see why Dixie had found what she wanted to take home from the beach. Boone Callahan could make a nun's panty hose creep down around her ankles. And that voice. Dixie had better be very careful.

"Likewise," Jill said. "Can you help us?"

"Honey, I don't think you can go to a fancy dress affair in one of my T-shirts even if they are the crème de la crème of all T-shirts," Boone said.

"No, we want to know where to go. We don't know anyone other than Faith, who knows someone named Jackson Smith, but we didn't think he'd know anything about shops since he's only here for the summer too. Uncle Vincent said—" Dixie was cut off.

"Jackson Smith? Vincent Galaway?" Boone raised an eyebrow.

"That's right," Dixie nodded.

"And you are going to work for me at minimum wage eighteen hours a week?" A cold chill raced up his back. Who'd he been kidding? Himself, for sure. She'd just been pulling his chain for thinking she was shoplifting. Teacher? That was probably a lie, too. She was a multimillionaire who lit cigarettes with thousand dollar bills.

"Why shouldn't I?" Dixie felt the chill from his voice. One minute he was warm and calling them darlin' and honey, the next a solid sheet of ice covered him like a winter coat.

"If you're acquainted with Jackson and Vincent, who

are by the way the richest men in these parts, then why would you be working at a T-shirt shop on the strip in Pensacola, Florida?" he asked bluntly.

"Jackson is rich?" Jill blurted out. "Wait until I tell Faith."

"We know Uncle Vincent is rich. Faith said he is and not every man in the world can afford to give fifty thousand dollars to a charity, but that doesn't mean we're rich, Boone Callahan," Dixie said. Finally, she realized what happened. He thought she was making a fool of him, applying for a job when she was running in rich circles.

"Uncle Vincent?" Boone asked.

"He's Faith's uncle. That's our other teacher friend from Arkansas. We just call him that because she does," Jill explained, still in the dark as to why sparks were flying between Dixie and Boone.

"There is an exclusive little shopping district about a mile down the strip. Turn right at the . . ." he counted the red lights in his head, ". . . the third red light. You'll see it sitting right over there on the left. A shop called Miss Laura's."

"Thank you so much," Jill said. "Come around to the beach house sometime. We'll be there all summer and you are Dixie's boss and all."

"Maybe I will," Boone narrowed his eyes at Dixie. "Can I really expect you to show up for work tomorrow morning or is this a mean little joke?"

"Oh, darlin', I'll be here with bells on my toes. Any other dress code I might need to follow?" Dixie shot right back at him. How dare the man judge her!

"Shorts are fine. Sandals or sneakers. Anything comfortable. No air conditioning as you can see. And here's your first work shirt. I painted it last night," he handed her an olive green shirt, almost the same color as her eyes.

She unfolded it carefully and spread it out on the counter beside the cash register. Ocean View T-shirts was dry brushed across the front with a smaller version of the same scene she'd bought the day before. Then her name was across the left side in fancy script lettering.

"I hope your name really is Dixie and you weren't feeding me a line," Boone said.

"It's Dixie all right and thanks for the shirt," she said.

"I'll have a couple more tomorrow. One for each day you work so you don't have to do laundry so often," he told her, hoping she was being honest with him.

"I'll be here at nine o'clock. And thank you again for the shopping advice," Dixie refolded her shirt and joined Jill in the Jeep.

"Can you believe that Faith just happened to fall into a relationship with another rich man?" Jill used her sunglasses to brush her bangs back from her forehead.

"Birds of a feather, you know," Dixie checked for traffic and pulled out.

"Your Boone is right easy on the eyes," Jill said.

"Looks like he's going to be a pain in the posterior," Dixie said. "He thought I was a rich woman playing a trick on him with the job because he'd accused me of shoplifting."

"You got all that from what he said?" Jill leaned her

head back on the headrest. She dreaded going to the bachelor auction but every nerve in her body exploded with more excitement than she'd known in years.

"Not from what he said. From his body language and the vibes," Dixie said.

"I didn't get anything like that," Jill said. "But then I was just entranced by the whole package. Now that's something worth taking home, Dixie."

"Then you take him home. I'm just going to work for him," Dixie snapped.

"Not me, darlin'," Jill did a perfect imitation of Boone's Texas drawl then giggled. "I'm going to take home a rich bachelor from Nawleans, sugar."

"You'd better work on that accent a little," Dixie laughed.

They found the dress at Miss Laura's. A scarlet sheath slit up to the thigh on one side, sequin covered spaghetti straps, a draping back that dipped down below bustline. Miss Laura herself suggested a backless bra and high-heeled sandals with only three skinny sequined straps to hold them on Jill's feet.

"So do we go out and celebrate having found the dress and all the trimmings with some lunch and a bottle of wine?" Dixie asked, helping Jill lay the dress out in the backseat of the Jeep.

"No, we go home and find out if Faith knows her boy toy is rich," Jill said. "Besides I bought a couple of pounds of shrimp from the fish man across the street from the house yesterday and Faith promised us gumbo for lunch," Jill said. "Then I'm going to lie on the beach and try to get a bit of brown on all this white flesh before I go to the big hoo-raw tomorrow."

"No you are not. Not one bit of tan. Your skin looked all creamy and translucent in that dress. Don't you dare risk a sunburn and ruin the effect," Dixie scolded her. "You can lie on the beach if you cover yourself in number nine hundred sun screen."

"Yes, ma'am, and if I take my nap can I get a piece of candy from the jar?" Jill stuck her finger in her mouth.

"Oh, stop it. Sarcasm will get you nowhere," Dixie said.

Faith was just adding the flour, a third of a tablespoon at a time to the hot oil when Jill and Dixie arrived. She stirred constantly, adding flour slowly until the roux was a thick brown substance, ready for the vegetables she'd already diced.

"We found the dress and we found out your new feller is rich," Jill unsheathed the dress and held it up for her to look at. "What is that horrid mess?"

"It's roux. I don't have file powder or okra so we'll have to make do, but it's going to be gumbo, and that dress is absolutlely stunning. Uncle Vincent will be the most popular man at the bachelor auction," Faith added vegetables to the roux and stirred gently.

"I thought every Cajun recipe began with 'melt a stick of butter'," Dixie said.

"It does. Only this one calls for a thick brown flour and oil mixture and then a stick of butter," Faith laughed. "And if there're leftovers I'm taking a bowl over to Jackson's house. What were you saying about him being rich?"

"Boone said he was rich," Dixie said. "But when you're a schoolteacher a ditch digger makes more money than you do and everyone looks rich."

"Oh, he's rich all right. Designs these games for kids and makes mega bucks. Travels everywhere. This is just his summer playground. He likes Switzerland in the winter and homebases out of a place called Marion, Virginia, where he says he was the high school nerd. I'm finding that a bit hard to believe, though," Faith tasted the end of the spoon and shook in more thyme, oregano, and another dash of cayenne.

"What's in this?" Dixie pointed toward a bowl of red liquid.

"That would be chicken stock, clam juice, tomato sauce, and a cup of white wine. And that would be shrimp, sausage, and chicken," she nodded toward a plate of diced meat and shelled shrimp.

"It smells so good I'm thinking I should have bought the bigger size in that dress," Jill eyed the creation hanging from the curtain rod in the dining room.

"Did you make double? I have a little bit of anger hiding in my soul," Dixie said.

"Oh no," Faith pressed the back of her hand across her forehead comically.

"She and her honey pie, Boone Callahan, had a disagreement. He thought she was pulling his leg about coming to work for him. A get-you-back for thinking she was shoplifting kind of thing." Jill opened a long loaf of French bread and began to slice it diagonally so she could butter it.

"I've already mixed the garlic butter," Faith said. "Now tell me more. Do I need to chop up some more vegetables?"

"No, I think that potful might be enough. I'm not really good and mad like I was when Todd proposed. Just enough that it'll take more than one bowlful to put me in a good mood. Remember while you're off with your rich man Jackson," she pointed at Faith, "and you're off in that dreamy dress seducing rich bachelors from New Orleans," she shifted her pointing to Jill, "that I'm going to be working my fingers to the bone in a T-shirt sweat shop."

"Poor, poor baby. I feel so sorry for you. Having to look at something like Boone all day long. And no air-conditioning, either. Maybe he'll get all sweaty and those muscles will shine and he'll mop his brow with the back of his hand and . . ." Jill intoned in mock sympathy.

"And now you can hush," Dixie said.

"No, I want to hear more. Is he really that good look-ing?" Faith asked.

"No, he's even better. Dixie could have him for breakfast, dinner, and supper and still be hungry for more," Jill laughed.

"On a mad day?" Faith asked, tucking her chin back and widening her eyes.

"On a day when Todd flies down and tells her that she's a dried up old maid," Jill said.

"I gotta meet this man. I might trade in my computer guru for him," Faith stirred and tasted.

"I might let you if he's as bullheaded tomorrow as he has been today. Is that about ready? I'm starving." Dixie watched Faith add the shrimp, sausage, and chicken to the bubbly mixture.

"Three minutes. That's the final step and shrimp only takes three minutes in boiling gumbo or it'll be tough. Get ready to feast, my friends," Faith watched the clock.

That afternoon Jill grabbed a bottle of sunscreen and a book and went down the back steps to the beach. Faith disappeared with a covered bowl of leftover gumbo, and Dixie found herself on the screened back porch with a thick romance novel, something she only allowed herself to indulge in during the summer months. While school was in session she read and reread Shakespeare, English literature, American literature and kept her grammar skills honed to a fine edge. The book had a scantily clad woman draped over the arms of a muscular man on the front. The English Duke had blond hair worn a bit longer than Boone's and crystal clear blue eyes, but the muscles were the same. The angles of his face were identical to Boone's, causing Dixie to wonder if her new boss might have a different sideline business posing for the front covers of steamy romances.

"That's crazy," she shook off the vision and opened the book. Twenty pages later she laid it aside, not remembering one word she'd read. Should she go in tomorrow morning and tell the man she'd had a change of heart? That she wanted a whole summer of nothing but sun, novels and gumbo. No, she wouldn't do that. She couldn't. She was already bored to insanity after only three days. On any other vacation, it would be time to go home now. Or just about. No, she was going to work part-time. She'd rat-hole the money to do something spectacular. Buy that new recliner she'd been coveting at the furniture store over in Conway. Or maybe a big screen TV.

It was only for six hours, she reminded herself. Six hours of the busiest time of the day and it would go fast. Then she'd rush home and she and Faith would give Jill the full beauty treatment. Faith would work some magic on all that long black hair, tying it up in something that looked like it came out of New York City. And Dixie would be in charge of the manicure and pedicure. When Jill walked through the door of the bachelor auction every head would turn and they'd wonder who the mystery lady was.

By the time Dixie got home on Saturday afternoon, Jill would be awake and ready to talk about the whole party—the dresses, the bachelors, the extravagance, how much money the auction raised. How it felt to be picked up and delivered in a long limo.

Will I ever wear a dress like that and go somewhere worthy of it with Boone? she asked herself in the middle of her fast moving planning for the next two days.

"Oh, for crying out loud. I just got out of a relationship with a suds-in-the-bucket kind of man. What makes me think he'll be any different? It's a rebound thing. Todd is all wrong for me and I know it, but I want someone in my life to fill the void." She slung the book on the floor, changed into her bikini without covering it up with the shirt she'd bought from Boone—she sure didn't need anything to see his face or body in vivid detail—and went to the beach.

She'd fry all those crazy thoughts from her mind. Because at the end of the summer all she was taking home was a pretty seashell, and that was pure fact that could be written down as the gospel according to Dixie.

Chapter Four

Dixie brushed her hair back from her sweating forehead and rang up a sale to a short gray-haired woman
who explained that the twelve T-shirts were for her
grandchildren; seven mermaids for the girls and five
beach scenes with surfboards stuck in the sand for the
boys. Dixie smiled and said the right things and looked
up to see who was next.

"Hi, we want to talk to the painter you got hired," a
teenage girl said in a conspiratorial whisper. "See, I
told you he was the most handsome thing on the whole
strip," she turned to her four friends.

"Go right on back there and tell him what you want
him to paint on your shirts," Dixie grinned. Boone was
in the middle of an order for fifteen identical shirts for
a group of women from Nebraska who were involved
in some kind of makeup convention. All hot pink with

the same beach scene. The only differences in the shirts were the names on the upper left-hand side and the sizes. A little hero worship in the middle of a mundane job would be good for him. She watched all five girls, not a day older than fifteen, strut back to the work area, trying to act older but their perfectly smooth baby complexions yelled they were barely out of puberty.

"Help you ladies?" Boone asked without stopping his work.

"We want some shirts. We're friends, see. And we want them all just alike. Something with a big, hunky man on the front, maybe lyin' out on the beach in a Speedo," the most brazen one said. "Maybe someone like you."

"Talk to Dixie up at the cash register. She takes the orders. Payment in advance for special orders. She's got a book of favorites. I think what you want is under the 'Ladies Only' section," Boone said. He put up with a score of flirty teenagers every day. The frequently asked questions included if they could watch him paint, if they could buy him a drink after work hours, if they could have his autographed picture or if he'd pose for a picture with one or all of them. He wondered for the millionth time where these girls' fathers were. If he had a daughter, she wouldn't be out on the strip wearing nothing but a bikini with so little material it wouldn't even sag a clothesline, much less flirting with a man old enough to be their father. Okay, okay, he argued with himself, he would have had to be nineteen when he fathered the child, but still it wasn't an impossibility.

"But we want *you* to show us. The lady up there

won't fire you if you take a minute to show us your work. If she does my daddy will give you a job in his factory in San Francisco," the girl said slyly.

Lord, this one was even more brazen than the others. He shot a look at Dixie who was leaning back against the bar and grinning. He'd fire her. At the end of the day he'd take her day's wages from the cash register and send her packing.

"Ladies," she called to the girls. "I do believe Mr. Callahan is much too busy to stop. Those shirts were due an hour ago and the women who've ordered them will be here soon. Come on up here and I'll help you decide what you want to purchase. So you're from San Francisco? What are you doing here? There're beaches in California, aren't there? And have you been down to Miss Laura's to do some shopping? She's got the most fabulous little evening gowns like you'd wear on a midnight cruise," Dixie lured them to the front of the store easily. Treat them like adults. Ask questions about them and talk about shopping. Worked every time. If it did fail, ask them about what kind of makeup they used. But she didn't have to resort to the last measure.

"Isn't he dreamy? Didn't I tell you he was the most handsome thing in the world. I'd ask him to let me buy him a drink if he wasn't so busy," the talker in the group said barely above a whisper as they looked through the book Dixie handed them.

"You old enough to buy drinks?" Dixie asked, pointing to a caricature of a hunky man holding up a surfboard.

"Of course," the girl giggled. "I'm twenty-one if I use my fake ID."

"That could get you in lots of trouble," Dixie warned.

"Only if I get caught and then Daddy will just laugh and pay the fine," the girl said.

"Not that kind of trouble," Dixie tried to be gentle and yet make the girl think.

"Oh, don't preach at us," one of the others said. "You're too old to appreciate a good looking man like that. I think we'll take this one. Five of them. All extra small size. And put the picture up high as it will go because we'll cut the bottoms off so our navel rings will show. Put our names on the surfboards. Should we use our real names or our girlfriend names?"

"Oh, our girlfriend names," a third one clapped her hands together. "We'll have our pictures taken in them all together."

"Names?" Dixie picked up a pencil and wrote out the order.

"Exquisite, Gorgeous, Fantastic, Beautiful, and Ravishing," the first one said. "Those are our full girl-friend names. We shorten them when we're talking to one another. I'm Rav, this is Ex, that's Gorge, next is Fan and that's Beaut."

"Very original," Dixie fought the muscles in her cheeks to keep from literally cracking up. "That will be twenty-five dollars plus tax for each shirt."

"Do you take American Express? I'll pay for all of them," Rav said as she produced plastic.

"Of course," Dixie ran the card through and pushed the tab across the bar for Rav to sign. "The shirts will be ready at two-thirty."

"We'll be here. Tell the good looking hunk he can

look forward to it. You got scissors here so we can cut them off? We'll even model them for him and maybe he'll take me up on that drink," Rav winked at Dixie.

"No scissors here, honey. My eyesight is failing so bad, my hired help back there is afraid I'll cut my fingers on them," she said seriously.

Ex sighed. "Look what we've got in our future, girlfriends—old age, wrinkles, and near blindness. We'd better have fun while we can."

Beaut patted her on the shoulder as they walked away. "But it's a long way off. I bet Dixie here is all of thirty years old. That means we're only halfway there."

Dixie turned quickly and covered her mouth to keep most of the laughter from floating down the strip to the girls' ears. She found herself only inches from Boone's chest, looking up into his twinkling brown eyes.

"No scissors, huh? Didn't you want to see what they'd look like with their little belly button decorations shining?" he said in his slow Texas drawl.

"I was busy saving your sorry hide from jail. After all, I'm so old and senile I wouldn't even know how to hail a taxi to take me to post bail for you. The shop would close down because with my arthritic hands I couldn't ever paint, and all those hunky muscles would go to flab in a jail cell," she said between guffaws. "Lord, how did you ever get any work done with such clients?"

"That's why I need help," he grinned. "You handled them very well, by the way. And here are the makeup conventions shirts. Don't tell me the diva dolls wanted pink too. I'm sick of painting on pink."

"Oh, yes, darlin'. Only it's a different shade and much much smaller. Extra small, they said. So it will stretch across what gravity hasn't laid claim to yet. Of course when they are really old, with one foot on a boiled okra pod and the other already in a freshly dug grave, like when they're about thirty, they'll clutch that shirt to their sagging bosom and remember the days of their glorious youth," she told him, backing away to get away from the sheer heat of the moment. They'd been right about one thing. He was good looking and he did throw off enough sex appeal to make a woman's knees weak. Didn't matter if she had a navel ring or varicose veins or anything in between.

"Modern day Shakespeare and I didn't even know I'd hired a poet," he said. "Thanks, Dixie, for steering the bunch of them back to the front. I can't imagine where their fathers are or why they let them run wild."

"You wouldn't turn your daughters loose like that?" she joked, choosing five pink shirts from the right bin and carrying them to the back.

"I don't have any daughters. Only nieces. But if they went anywhere with clothes on like that, I'd wrap them in a gunny sack and put them in a convent. They'd be grounded for eternity plus three days," Boone looked at the picture of the cartoonish man with a surfboard, stretched a T-shirt over a board and went to work. "What on earth do these names mean?"

"They stand for Exquisite, Gorgeous, Fantastic, Beautiful, and Ravishing. Those are their girlfriend club names," she told him, taking a moment to watch him work since there were no other customers.

"Egotistical little critters, ain't they?" He laughed.

"Sons? You got sons? Would you let them run up and down the boardwalk in their little Speedos?" she asked.

"Got no sons, either. Only nephews. And no, I would not. What's good for the goose is good for the gander. To dash off to the snow cone stand or ice cream joint to get something cold to drink in your bathing suit is one thing. To wear a bikini that barely covers the essentials to go shopping is another," he told her as he worked.

"Married?" she asked.

"No. Not now. Never have been. Intend to some day, but not now. Got three brothers. Crock is the oldest. Then Bowie and then Houston right next to me. They're all married. Crock's got three kids, all boys. Bowie has two daughters. Houston has two of each."

"Strange names," Dixie said.

"Not any stranger than Rav, Ex, and Fan." He produced the scene on the front of the shirt with very little effort. "My folks were quite taken with the story of the Alamo. Crock is David Crockett Callahan. Bowie is James Bowie. Houston is as you've already guessed, Sam Houston. By the time I was born they had a choice: they could name me for Santa Ana or else forget the Alamo. Now, honey, no one in Texas forgets the Alamo, and they weren't about to name me for a pompous man like Santa Ana, thank goodness, so they decided that if Daniel Boone had been called upon to come save the Alamo then history could have been written differently. So yes, I am Daniel Boone Callahan. And I've lived my whole life under the shadow of my brothers, who's namesakes really did fight at the Alamo," he laid one shirt aside and started the next one.

Before Dixie could answer a dozen tired women arrived to lay claim to their shirts. Middle-aged, some with gray hair, but their makeup was perfect. Not one stepped up with plastic and offered to pay for the whole lot of shirts. Dixie guessed generosity was in short supply when Daddy didn't pay the bills. While the last one paid and Dixie made change a man wandered through the door, looking at the shirts already on display.

"Help you, sir?" she asked.

"Yes, you could go to dinner with me tonight," he smiled showing off perfect white teeth in a tanned face. Thick gray hair had been cut in a feathered back style and crystal blue eyes glittered.

"Sorry, can't date customers. House rule," she said flippantly.

"Honey, I'd make a rule like that too if I was married to you," the man nodded toward Boone, who kept working but didn't miss a word that was said.

"Oh, I'm not married to Boone. I just work for him. See anything you'd like to buy?" she asked, changing the subject.

"Yes, ma'am. I'd buy you in a minute," he said. "But since you're not for sale, I'll take these two shirts. I'm Morgan Chase and I live in the area. Have a little hotel up the beach a ways. I'll stop by and see if I can change your mind about that dinner every few days."

"Thank you, but no thanks. I'll ring up these shirts, though," Dixie told him. Sure he was good looking, well built in a lanky yet muscular way. Tall, not muscular like Boone, but not saggy like his gray hair would suggest.

"I'm divorced for the past ten years. I'm forty-five years old. Have a twenty-two-year-old daughter and a six-month-old grandson. I'm not a kook and I don't usually ask sales clerks out to dinner," he said as he produced a credit card.

"That's quite a pick-up line. Don't know that I've heard it before," she handed him back the card.

"It's not a line. If I'm lyin', I'm flyin', honey, and my feet ain't left the ground," Morgan told her. "You look like you'd be an interesting dinner date."

"Thank you again," Dixie almost blushed. At least he didn't think she was old and about to need the services of an undertaker.

"I'll be back," he promised as another bunch of teenagers flooded the shop. This time the teens were interested in instant gratification. What was on the rack, already painted, and they didn't even want their names painted anywhere on them.

"So why didn't you go out with Morgan?" Boone brought the girlfriend club's shirts to the front.

"You know him?" Dixie asked.

"I don't know him but I know of him. He owns a little exclusive hotel up the beach a half a mile or so. It's only two floors and has about fifty suites. Most expensive place to stay on the whole strip. He's legitimate, Dixie," Boone said.

"Wonder if the rich little girlfriends would think he was a hunk?" she asked.

Boone threw back his head and guffawed. "I doubt it.

Not with gray hair and wearing one of his business suits."

"How come it is that you get hit on by the youth and only the Geritol generation is interested in me?" she asked.

"Class, darlin'," he said. "You got class and if Geritol is Morgan's secret, I'm going to start bathing in it."

The rest of the day went rapidly. A steady line of customers kept Boone painting and Dixie busy selling from the racks and ringing up sales. When the sassy little girls arrived still in their skimpy bikinis, their young bodies well oiled and sweaty from a day of sun worship, she couldn't believe it was already two-thirty.

"So where's the painter?" Rav asked, producing a brand new pair of scissors from her beach bag and cutting away the bottom of her shirt.

"Coffee break," Dixie said, wondering herself where he had disappeared to.

"Oh, look, aren't we going to be sexy," Rav pulled the shirt over her head, the bottom of the surfboard looking like it did indeed rise right out of her taut little stomach. A navel ring with a string of three little diamonds danced right at the end of the board.

"Ahhhh," the other four said in unison, passing their shirts to Rav for alterations.

"Let's take out the sleeves, too," Ex suggested.

Rav nodded, removing her shirt in one swift motion. By the time the girls left, the shirts were short and sleeveless. Dixie wondered why they hadn't just gone to the tattoo parlor and had the caricature of the hunk permanently laid upon their chests.

She made sure they were a block away before she went looking for Boone. The bathroom, a tiny closet-like room was at the back of the shop. Barely room for a toilet and a wall-hung sink, but immaculately clean. The door was open so he wasn't in there. The closet door beside it was shut tight. Surely, she reasoned with herself, he didn't hide in the closet every time a bit of fluffy jailbait came into the shop.

She had her hand up about to knock when the door swung outward. She had to jump aside to avoid having it hit her square in the face.

"Oh, I'm sorry," Boone apologized. "I was making a pot of coffee. Have to admit, I did it on purpose when I saw that gaggle of giggles coming to get their shirts. Oh, I forgot to tell you this morning. Noticed you ate a sandwich you'd brought along in between customers. We do have a kitchen. It's a remodeled closet," he stepped aside and gave her the five second tour.

"Stove top with two burners, refrigerator, and sink all in one. Shelf for the microwave, toaster, and coffee pot. Another shelf for a loaf of bread or cookies. I usually make a sandwich sometime during the day. You're welcome to use any of it. As you can see though, it's too small for two people. So when Rav and her friends come, it's mine," he said.

"Deal. And when old men come to ask this classy woman out, it's mine," she told him. "It's three. My shift is up."

"See you tomorrow morning," he said.

"I'll be here," she gathered up the brown paper bag and her purse and left him standing there at the cash register.

A mature woman with a sense of humor, he thought as he watched her walk away until she melted into the crowds and disappeared. The little girls hadn't fazed her with their insensitive comments, but then she was a high school English teacher. She dealt with the likes of them every day. Crock would yell at him for not asking her out to dinner; for putting a plug in for Morgan Chase. Bowie would frown and tell him he was a complete idiot to have such a woman right next to him all summer and to let her get away on the first day without at least a little flirting. Houston? Oh, my, Houston the lawyer would talk until his ears hurt about how foolish he was. Boone liked the way Dixie worked. The way she kept her cool in all kinds of situations and she was attractive. But he wasn't going to jeopardize the best help he'd ever had for a few kisses.

When Dixie arrived home she found Faith and Jill in a flurry of preparations. Jill had already had a long bubble bath with oils. Sitting at the kitchen table in a white terry cloth bathrobe, Faith was blow-drying her long dark hair. Crimson finger nail polish, along with all the tools of the trade stood ready on the table beside her.

"Okay, you're twenty minutes late and the limo is going to be here in an hour. So you'd better drop that bag, get the dreamy look out of your eyes and get busy," Faith said.

"That's a lot to ask just minutes after she's left her Texas honey," Jill said.

"He's not my Texas honey. Prop your feet up here," Dixie pulled a chair over in front of Jill. "We'll do toenails first."

"Married is he?" Jill asked.

"No. I did ask. Not now and never has been. He's the baby of four boys. Their parents might not have raised them right either," Dixie picked up the clippers and started her job.

"Rich? Thinks he's God?" Jill asked.

"No, that's Jackson," Dixie said.

"Hey, we're not talking about Jackson. He is rich but he doesn't think he's God. He was the high school nerd who made it big," Faith told them.

"Then what is it?" Jill asked.

"He really is Daniel Boone Callahan. His brothers are David Crockett. They call him Crock. And Sam Houston or Houston. Then there's James Bowie and they call him Bowie," Dixie said.

"True old Texans," Faith said. "Nothing wrong with that."

"You don't think so?" Dixie raised a dark eyebrow.

"We need to wax your eyebrows when we finish Jill. You're beginning to look shaggy again," Faith said.

"So he's not married and you didn't ask him to come by later for a midnight swim on our part of the beach?" Jill asked. "Sounds to me like your periapt is working fine. And you promised that mine wouldn't work tonight, Faith."

"It won't. You'll find a rich southern man who'll melt at your feet when he sees your beauty and your periapt isn't going to keep you from one bit of mischief. I promise. Dixie's isn't working either, but it's like the blond and the lottery ticket. Remember that story?" Faith began to work her magic on Jill's long black hair, twirling it up on top of her head in an arrangement of exotic curls.

"Refresh my memory," Jill said.

"The blond prayed one night that she'd win the lottery. She didn't. So not giving up her faith, she prayed the next week that she'd win it. She didn't. So she prayed longer and harder that she'd win the lottery. After six weeks, she was on her knees praying again when a loud booming voice came down from the sky saying, 'If you want to win, you've got to buy a ticket.' That's Dixie. If she wants to get into mischief she has to put in some effort. It doesn't always just come and jump on your toes. You've got to work at it a little. You've got to try to steal three T-shirts."

"I wasn't shoplifting," Dixie grumbled.

"Like you and Jackson," Jill asked. "What did you do to attract him to you that night?"

Faith laughed. "That darlin' is my business. But rest assured when I saw him walking down the beach, I sure enough got his attention."

"Faith Galaway!" Jill exclaimed.

"Well, I did. And if Dixie wants to take Boone home with her, she'll have to find a way to get into a little bit of mischief. Now tell us more about him. How was it working in that sweat shop with him all day?" Faith asked.

Dixie kept them laughing with her stories of the fabulous five, as she'd nicknamed the young girls, until the limo arrived.

"Oh, my, now I'm nervous," Jill said.

"No need to be, honey. You're the mystery lady. Not a single soul knows you. Bid on Uncle Vincent then buy yourself a young, good looking feller and flirt like hell," Faith told her. "Oh, and you can tell Dixie all about it but remember the details until Sunday. Jackson and I are doing one of those wicked little weekend cruises. We're leaving at eight tonight and we'll be home on Sunday evening."

"Have fun," Jill said, shaking her head.

"Stop shaking your head at me. You'll ruin your hair. And rest assured, I know what I'm doing. It's just a fun summer. Nothing serious. He's just good for fun and that's all I'm interested in," Faith told them both.

"You have fun," Dixie gave Jill an easy hug, careful not to muss her dress or mess up her makeup.

"I'm not sure I remember how to have fun in a setting like this, but I'm going to do my best," Jill climbed into the limo.

Later that evening, Dixie watched the sun set over the ocean. The bright oranges, pinks and grays blending together in a wild array of natural color that rendered her breathless. Faith had packed a suitcase with everything but the kitchen sink. Jill was off hobnobbing with the millionaires and she didn't envy either of them. She had the best of the world sitting there in the warm white sugar sands, watching the orange ball of light slowly dip on the far horizon.

She wondered if Boone came walking down the beach right then what kind of mischief she'd conjure up to get him to notice her. She couldn't think of a single thing. It might be that even though she was physically attracted to him that a good solid friendship was all that destiny was going to offer. Besides, she'd just shut the door on a year-long relationship and she sure didn't need to jump right into another one.

Maybe she would go out with Morgan Chase. Just to get Todd out of her soul and heart. Yes, she decided, as she brushed the sand from her rather modest bikini, she would go to dinner with the man if he did indeed come back into the shop. Dinner didn't mean commitment, and it sure didn't mean that she was putting the battery back in her biological clock.

Chapter Five

Dixie and Jill were playing scrabble on the coffee table when Faith arrived home Sunday near midnight. She dragged her suitcases into the foyer and shut the door, leaving them until morning to unpack.

"So the prodigal finally comes back to the farm," Jill teased. "Is Jackson going to get into trouble for breaking curfew?"

"No jokes. I'm miserable. I think I've got a fever and I must have been allergic to the shrimp or something. I've got this rash," Faith pulled up her shirt and showed them her belly.

"Rash?" Dixie jumped up and examined the red dots. "That's not a rash girl. That's a full-blown case of chicken pox. When did you first notice the bumps?"

"Chicken pox!" Faith groaned. "I must have contracted them the last day of school. There were a couple of students who had them. Oh, Lord, this is awful, and they itch so bad."

"Don't scratch," Jill told her. "Don't even think about it. We'll go get some Aveeno to put in your bath tomorrow and some lotion to keep them from itching."

"Even some anti-itch pills, but tonight you'll just have to endure," Dixie said. "How on earth did you ever escape chicken pox as a child?"

"I went to private boarding school. The head mistress was so mean that no childhood disease would dare enter her school. She was Marie Leveau reincarnated. I can't believe I have chicken pox at thirty-five. There has to be some kind of genetic law against this," Faith moaned.

"There is. It's called growing up poor in public schools where all childhood diseases run rampid," Dixie said. "My brothers and I had them when I was about six."

"I wish I'd been your friend then and know what I know now. Oh, damn," Faith said. "Jackson. I bet I gave them to him."

"Not to worry," Jill soothed her. "He's probably already had them, too."

"Am I the only woman in the world who's not had them? And how long do these horrible things last?" Faith asked.

"Ten days to two weeks. If you don't scratch you might escape any scars," Dixie said. "Now go take a shower and soap them up good. That dries them somewhat and we'll get medicine soon as the nearest pharmacy opens tomorrow."

"Scars?" Faith screwed up her face. "Am I going to have to pay for plastic surgery?"

"Not if you don't scratch," Dixie reminded her.

"Hurry up. We've got things to tell you," Jill said.

Five minutes later Faith was back in the living room, wrapped in one towel, another fashioned into a turban for her hair, barefoot and dripping onto the carpet. "They are in my ears and on my face. Not to mention other places too sensitive to scratch. Have these things no mercy? A summer of fun my hiney. This is a summer straight from the bowels of hell itself."

"Sit down here," Jill motioned toward the sofa. When Faith had plopped down dramatically, throwing the back of her hand across her forehead in true southern disgust, Jill tucked a thin sheet around her all the way to her armpits, then wrapped her hands in a couple of soft pillowcases.

"I feel like a mummy," Faith said. "Is this one of the seven plagues mentioned in the Good Book?"

"Who knows? We just have to keep you from scratching until morning. Then we'll get medicine and you'll be all groggy for the rest of the time and won't remember a thing about them in a couple of years," Dixie said.

"I can't be groggy. I won't take it. Jackson will find another playmate if I'm groggy. He won't like me anymore. Oh, damn, we were going to play miniature golf tomorrow night," Faith reached up to scratch her nose but the pillowcase stopped her. "They itch worse than fire ant bites."

"I remember," Dixie said, "Momma said if I

scratched I'd never get a husband. I think maybe she was right."

"Entertain me. Tell me about your weekend. Did you find a rich man?" Faith looked at Jill.

"I did. A very nice rich man. He's not so much to look at. About my height. Not muscular like Boone. Not skinny, though. We're going out to dinner Friday night. He's in Mobile for the week and I'm meeting him there. I may spend the weekend in a hotel there rather than drive back late at night. He's called twice already. We may have dinner on Friday and go over to New Orleans on Saturday to tour the French Quarter," Jill said.

"Are you going to take him home?" Faith asked.

"Who knows? It's much too early to tell," Jill smiled, her whole face radiating.

Dixie had never seen Jill look like that before. She'd dated lots of men in and around Conway and Greenbrier but never had she actually blushed just talking about one.

"And you? Did your Boone ask you out?" Faith asked.

"No, but Morgan Chase did. I guess he's a rich fish in this pond. I'm going to dinner with him tomorrow night. He's picking me up at eight," Dixie said.

"Has he had chicken pox?" Faith asked.

"I would imagine. He's forty-five years old. A grandfather and a divorcee," Dixie said.

"Good Lord, I get a boy toy and you get a sugar daddy," Faith giggled.

"I didn't get anything," Dixie told her. "I'm just going to dinner with him."

"And what does Daniel Boone think of that?" Faith asked.

"Boone doesn't think anything of it. It's none of his business. He's just my employer not my . . ." Dixie struggled for the right word.

"Not your Todd Riley," Faith said.

"I'll never waste another year on any man," Dixie said.

"Not even your sugar daddy? He might fall asleep during dinner? Don't kiss him too long or you could make his blood pressure rise so high he'll stroke out," Faith teased.

"I deserve that after all the things I've said about Jackson. Which brings me to wonder when we get to meet him. Or is he just a figment of your imagination?" Dixie asked.

"Oh, he's real all right. Kisses that melt my toenails. Gentle. Sweet. I could easily fall for him. But I'd have to admit that I'm ten years older than him. Put in the Ya-Ya's and let's watch it. Anything to keep my mind off these boils."

"Good Lord, Faith. They aren't boils. They're hardly bigger than pimples," Jill said.

"Depends on whether you're looking at them or living with them," Faith told her seriously.

"I may max out my credit card and spend the next two weeks in Mobile," Jill said.

"Oh, no, you aren't leaving me with this pox infested witch for two weeks all by myself," Dixie intoned.

"You can't afford to go to Mobile that long. She'd stay so mad at me she'd eat everything in sight and gain five hundred pounds and then you'd feel guilty," Faith said.

"The things we do for friends," Dixie said, putting in the DVD of *The Divine Secrets of the Ya-Ya Sisterhood*. She could relate to the women in the movie. Even if she and Jill and Faith hadn't known each other since childhood, had come from entirely different backgrounds, they were still as close as the women in the movie and probably always would be. So what if they were thirty-five and had a silly name for their friendship—the PMS Club. It wasn't one bit goofier than the Ya-Ya's.

By the movie's end they were all wiping tears and declaring that once a year was definitely enough to watch such a heart-wrenching movie.

"So what kind of mother will you make?" Dixie asked her friends.

"Probably one just like Viv and that's why I'm not having children," Faith said.

"You never told us that before," Jill drew down her eyebrows.

"That's because I just figured it out. When I was going with Travis all those years, I kept putting off the wedding. I wanted a summer wedding then when summer got here, I wanted a winter one with a white velvet gown and poinsettias in all the church windows. Before that I didn't want a wedding before I finished college. Any excuse would do, but now that I've had time to think about it, it's not that I didn't want to marry, it's that I didn't want to marry Travis and have the house full of kids he kept talking about. Just thinking about diapers and cleaning up vomit and slobbers while they're teething is enough to give me hives worse than chicken pox," Faith said.

"Is that why he reminded you so much of Todd?" Dixie asked.

"Yes, and the fact he's as rich as a king. When I told him I wasn't ready to have a family, that I wanted to play longer, he said we could hire a nanny but he'd expect me to be a mother. That's when my feet turned to ice and I backed out of the whole relationship," Faith said.

"Did you tell him why?" Jill asked.

"No, just told him that I wasn't ready to be tied down and a year later I came to Arkansas to get away from running into him every time I turned around," Faith told them.

"Well, I'm going to be a good mother if I ever get the chance to try it," Jill said. "I wanted children right after I married, but my husband said we should wait until we bought a house. An apartment was no place to raise kids, according to him. By the time we had the money for a down payment he'd died. I want a whole yard full of kids and I want to make cookies and raise them myself."

"Then you should marry Todd," Dixie said sarcastically.

"No, thank you. I can't stand that man, and I thought we weren't going to mention him all summer and here his name has already come up twice in ten minutes. He's too egotistical for me. I'd have his sorry carcass planted under the azalea bushes before we were married a week," Jill threw up her hands in mock horror.

"Don't look at me. I don't want your reject," Faith said when her friend glanced her way. "Friendship only goes so far and I don't want any kids, much less a house full of snotty nosed brats that all look like Todd Riley."

"But you would have loved my kids even if they'd been fathered by Todd?" Dixie asked.

"Sure," Jill and Faith both said.

"And I would have sent them expensive presents from afar and come to see you about once a decade," Faith said.

"And I would have offered to baby-sit for you and Todd to go away on vacations, but I wouldn't have come around if he was there," Jill said.

"And neither of you mentioned anything like this when I was dating him?" Dixie posed the question.

"You are our friend and we would have endured him for you," Jill patted her shoulder. "But we don't have to worry about that now do we?"

"I say we need a dose of honesty from now on," Dixie said. "If I don't like your Jackson when and if we ever get to meet the illusive little boy, I intend to tell you so right up front. And your rich feller, too," Dixie pointed at Jill.

"Deal. The PMS Club hereby writes into the rules and regulations that we must be honest. Now tell me truthfully that these evil boils only last twenty-four hours and I'll be able to play golf with Jackson tomorrow night," Faith said.

"Sorry, it's ten days to two weeks and then the scabs will take a while after that to fall off," Dixie said.

"Scabs! I thought you were teasing about the scabs. I

thought the boils would just disappear," Faith raised her voice in a high squeak.

"Honestly?" Jill said.

Faith nodded, unable to utter a word.

"Scabs," Dixie said with a yawn.

"Chicken pox!" Morgan had to suppress a chuckle.

"Yes, and she's dramatic at best and quite the over-done actress right now," Dixie looked over the menu in her hands. To say the restaurant was fancy would be a gross understatement. The tables were covered in white damask linen with oversized napkins to match. Pure white China with a fine gold rim were set on gold chargers. Crystal wine glasses cut so the facets picked up the candlelight from the center of the table. Dixie sat deep in a comfortable padded chair of white velvet with wide arms. It wasn't just a place to eat, but more a place to visit while eating.

"You are exceedingly lovely tonight, Dixie. That shade of crimson brings out the glow in your perfect complexion," Morgan said lazily from his side of the table.

High color filled her cheeks with more glow. She couldn't remember the last time she'd had a compliment like that. If she ever had. "Thank you, Morgan," she said, liking the way his name rolled off her tongue. "But I have to tell you, flattery will get you anything you want."

"Oh, really," he cocked his head to one side and grinned, those clear blue eyes lighting up like stars in a midnight sky.

"No, not really," she stammered.

"Of course, I was only teasing as you were," he said. "I'm glad you agreed to have dinner with me. This is the lonely part of the day for a single man. Mornings and afternoons are busy with the hotel. Evenings are often long affairs in front of the television watching news programs or reading. I suppose you suffer the same, though."

"Not me. I've got the chicken pox queen to keep entertained. And there's Jill who's met this fantastic rich man," Dixie blushed again. "I didn't mean that like it sounded. I'm not materialistic and a man doesn't have to have a bank account big enough to choke a Missouri mule for me to like him. But she's met this man and since she's been careful not to tell us his name yet, we call him the rich man. He has to have more money than Midas to run in circles with Uncle Vincent. That would be Faith's uncle, Vincent Galaway, not mine. Anyway, I don't have time for boredom."

"Vincent Galaway? That's the chicken pox queen's uncle. Good grief, he's one of my golfing buddies. When he's in town we always make time for a round. He's a very wealthy man." Morgan laid the menu aside.

"That's what they keep saying. I've never met him. Jill's been his mystery lady since we've been down here and since she's met Mr. Rich Man, I suppose she'll continue to be Uncle Vincent's escort for the charity events during the summer. That way she can see her new beau at the same time she is going with Uncle Vincent." Dixie laid her menu on top of Morgan's.

The waiter appeared as if on cue, his pencil poised

above a fancy notepad. "Have you made your decisions?" he asked.

"Yes, I have," Dixie said. "I'll have the crab cake appetizer, the house salad, and the lobster with hot butter sauce and baked potato with all the trimmings."

"Make that two," Morgan said. "And a bottle of your finest wine, please. You choose whatever you think will complement the meal we've chosen."

"So tell me about yourself, Dixie Nelson," Morgan said after the waiter left. "You come from Arkansas and you are a teacher. What else is there?"

"I'm just getting out of a year-long relationship with a man and I'm not interested in anything permanent right now. Thought I'd get that out and up front right away. I was born and raised in central Arkansas. Haven't been to a lot of places and have taught for twelve years. That's about it in a nutshell. Now tell me about you, Morgan," she said sipping at the cool water in crystal so thin she could have taken a bite right out of the side of the goblet.

"Divorced many years. My life got put on hold with my job and my wife and I grew apart. It was a friendly divorce. No ugly words. The marriage simply died in its sleep. We're still friends. My daughter always had both parents even if we didn't live together anymore. My ex-wife remarried an old boyfriend she'd had in high school many years before and is quite happy over in New Orleans. The rest has been work, eat, sleep, and start all over again and, occasionally, a dinner with a beautiful woman such as yourself. Nothing serious up to now. Maybe my luck is changing," he reached across the table and clinked his glass with hers, creating a tingly sound.

"That, kind sir, sounds like a pick up line to me." Dixie looked him right in the eye.

"Ah, the lady sees right through the ruse," Morgan grinned again. "Okay, truth. I've dated some women my age but most of them have a lot of baggage. A few your age, but not nearly as lovely, I might add, and that's not a pick up line. Any younger than you are and they tend to think about children, dogs, PTA, and a house with a yard. I've been there, done that. Wouldn't change any of it. But I'm not game to do it again. I would never start over again at my age. Three o'clock feedings and diapers are not in my future. I've found women in their mid-thirties, like you, are past that stage. They are established and comfortable in their own skin. They don't need constant reminders of their own beauty and worth and they're past that itch for motherhood."

The appetizers arrived. The dinner was delicious. The conversation after the ground rules were established quite stimulating. The kiss at the door of the beach house pleasant if not earth shaking.

Dixie leaned against the back of the door for a moment before she tiptoed to her room and donned her oldest one-piece bathing suit, threw the oversized T-shirt over it and went out the back door to the beach. She sat down in the sand and picked up a handful, letting it sift through her fingers. The lulling sound of the water sweeping in and out, plus the mesmerizing effect of the sand falling between her fingers and back to its home, almost hypnotized Dixie.

"Well, hello, what are you doing out here this late?" Boone asked from three feet away.

"I might ask the same of you," she brushed her hands together. Irritation filled her. In another minute she would have had her whole life planned. She would have resolved some unanswered questions and known what she wanted—why Todd still riled her so badly, why Morgan didn't appeal to her in spite of his charm and money.

"Couldn't sleep so I'm out for a midnight walk in the sand. It's soothing to the soul. Mind if I sit down?" he asked.

"It's a big beach. I sure can't tell you not to sit down, Boone. Where do you stay during the summer?" she asked.

"I park a small RV about a half a mile up the beach from here. Within walking distance of the T-shirt shop. That way I don't need a car all summer. I like your end of the beach. It's quieter down here with the houses and away from the hotels," he said. "So, what brings you out at this time of night? Waiting up for one of your friends?"

"No, I took your advice and went out with Morgan Chase tonight. He came into the shop Sunday afternoon while you were gone to get a corn dog. He asked me out to dinner and I accepted," she said honestly.

Boone held his breath. He honestly did not want to be attracted to this woman but he was. She was exactly the opposite of his ideal woman. The lady he'd marry someday and they'd have a whole yard full of children. The one who was at least five-foot-eight inches tall, had sweeping blond hair flowing down her back, big round blue eyes and was as graceful as a swan. Dixie Nelson was none of those things with her medium brown hair barely long enough to pull back into a ponytail. A round face with mischief in her mossy green eyes and just tall enough to reach his shoulder.

"Well, aren't you going to ask how the date went?" she said after a few minutes of silence.

"I suppose if you want to tell me, you will." A cold chill radiated from his voice.

"I won't be going out with him again," she said.

A whoosh of air left his lungs but he was careful to let it out slowly so she wouldn't hear. Holy smoke, he didn't care if she married the man. Or that's what he tried to convince himself right then.

"Why?" Boone scooped up wet sand into his hand and began to build a small sand castle.

"Because we want totally different things and it's a waste of time I don't have to encourage a relationship with him," she said.

"Maybe he doesn't want a relationship. Maybe he just wants a summer fling," Boone began to work on his castle in earnest.

"Well, I don't have time for summer flings. I'm not here to provide some man with a summer fling. I'd rather have a summer. . . . What are you building?" she asked.

"A castle for a maiden in distress to live in all summer. Where she can have a summer fling if she wants and then go home at the end of the summer with lots of beautiful memories," he teased.

"Moveover, that castle is not big enough for the maiden. She's going to need lots more room than that if she's to make enough memories to last a whole year," she laughed, forgetting all about Morgan and the heavy thoughts she'd been entertaining. "Is there a knight in shining armor who's going to ride by her castle on a white horse with a bright purple pome-thing-a-ma-bob on his head?"

"Of course, I wouldn't think of building a castle if I didn't have at least a knight in the background. But maybe the maiden is going to bypass all the knights and have a summer fling with the stable boy." He molded and fashioned the sand into turrets on the top of the pile they'd patted into submission.

"She might. She's pretty willful and she's found out money sure isn't everything," Dixie laughed.

Boone's heart soared and he had trouble roping it back in. They were just playing like little children, like his nieces and nephews did when they came to Pensacola during the first week of August every year. Playing a game called pretend that had nothing to do with reality.

"Are we talking about the maiden or are we talking about Dixie Nelson?" he asked, his hand brushing against hers during the construction of a magnificent sand castle.

"Who knows? It's a pretend game, Boone. Pretend this is the place where the maiden is kept because she wouldn't marry the Duke her father betrothed her to. Pretend this is the stable," she drew a square with her fingertip behind the castle, "and it's where the handsome stable boy lives."

"Pretend, huh?" Boone grinned.

"It's more fun than reality. When you get my age you're supposed to be settled and know where you are going in life. Be past the age when you want children and a house with a yard and PTA meetings. So we'll pretend and forget the real world. It's always there. Pretend is only here for a little while," she said, her voice so hauntingly sad it almost broke his heart.

"Want to talk about it?" He reached across the castle turret and took her sand-covered hand in his.

"No, I just want to live in a pretend world a little longer," she said, liking the way his big hand engulfed her small one. How on earth could a man with hands like that paint intricate pictures on T-shirts?

"It's your call," he dropped her hand and picked up another handful of wet sand to build his stable. "But the stable boy at least needs to have a nice place for them to meet when she can sneak out of the castle."

More emotion was stirred in that brief sharing of hands than had been when Morgan had kissed her good night. Another thing Dixie would have to ponder like a red-boned hound dog out on the tracks of a wily coyote. Maybe by the end of the summer she'd have everything figured out.

Chapter Six

Dixie straightened the T-shirts and swept sand from the bare wood floors for the fourth time that Sunday afternoon. They'd been so busy the past three days that she and Boone had scarcely exchanged a dozen words. Most of the time she pinned up the orders for more shirts on a line in his part of the shop and he simply nodded, if he even looked up at all. She could see where he would definitely need help during the weekends, and after four days of doing nothing but reading, sleeping and enjoying the beach with one date thrown in, she was more than ready to go to work that week.

"Dixie, could I ask a big favor?" He outlined a sailboat on the ocean with the sun setting on the horizon. "I'm still swamped. I've never been so busy in all the years I've been here. Could you stay until nine tonight. Pay you time and a half."

"Sure," she said, without taking her eyes from the pile of sand she'd accumulated in front of the broom. "The chicken pox queen is healing up nicely. By tomorrow or the next day she'll be out on the beach again. She's spent most of her time next door at Jackson's place anyway. He's been teaching her to play chess. And Jill has flown to some tropical paradise for a few days with her rich man so the house is empty anyway."

"Thanks," Boone said. "Not interrupting any hot dates then?"

"Sure, you are. My stable boy will just pine away," she said. "He may go back to Ireland—or was it Scotland?—with his heart shattered in a million pieces. He may never pose for a picture on the front of a steamy romance again. Or worse, he might never train horses in a sand castle again."

Boone laid the airbrush down and picked up a glass of iced tea. If she was staying until closing, some of the tension had alleviated. He'd get the orders out and start Monday morning with a fresh slate. He watched her carefully sweep the sand up into a dustpan. She'd sure enough proven her worth the past couple of weeks. He hadn't told her to keep things straightened or to sweep every day, but she did both.

"Seriously, Dixie. I wondered if you might have had a change of heart about Morgan?" he asked cautiously.

"No. He called a couple of times, but I'm not interested," she said.

"No summer flings for the maiden in distress even after we built her a perfect place to live?" He laid the shirt to one side to dry and picked up another. This one a child's size on which the buyer wanted a dolphin. He put a new tip on the airbrush and began to paint.

"The castle was washed plumb away the next morning. I think that game of pretend is over," she told him.

"Let's see, the old line in the movies was, 'What's a pretty girl like you doin' in a place like this?' isn't it?" Boone asked.

Dixie leaned over the partition keeping Boone and all his supplies neatly in their own cubby hole. "Sweeping sand up off the floor, can't you see? Tell you a secret, Boone. I just got out of a year-long relationship. I thought I loved the man but I was only in love with being in love. My biological clock sounded like Big Ben in my ears and I was rushing to find a suitable husband. It wouldn't be fair to Morgan or any other man right now. Rebound love is more fickle than no love."

Boone heard the honesty in her voice. "No pain?"

"More anger than pain. He took me for granted. Thought he'd just say the word and we'd rush off to the courthouse and get married. Not a thought about what I'd want in a wedding or if I'd marry him at all. I could stay home and raise his children and never have to lift a finger to work again. There'd be housekeepers, cooks, nannies, anything I wanted so why wasn't I licking his boots and sitting in the vault counting all his money?"

"And you turned that down?" Boone asked incredulously.

"You ever heard the song Sara Evans has out about suds in the bucket?" Dixie asked.

"Of course. You know what kind of music I listen to since you are right here all weekend. What's that got to do with your story?" Boone asked.

"Well, Todd Riley wanted me to be a suds-in-the-bucket kind of woman. It's complicated and I'd bore you to snoring with it. Go on back to your work," she said.

"What kind of woman is that? A suds-in-the-bucket kind of woman? I don't hear that in the song. I hear a young girl running off so fast she didn't even finish the washing so she could be with the love of her life," Boone painted an eye on the dolphin, giving it character and life.

"That's what Todd heard too, and that's what the song is all about, I'm sure. But I heard it on the radio when we were fighting. I got a vision of Todd I didn't like. He wants me to be a mealy mouthed little woman who never speaks her mind. Who lives to keep his coffee cup filled because he says so, not because I want to do those things. It's hard to put into words. He wants a woman that'll do the laundry on the back porch. I want a man who'll be happy with a brand new automatic washing machine. One that lets me be myself. That loves me for what I am. That doesn't want to change anything about me. I want kids. I want a husband and a house with a yard. PTA, chicken pox, a career as a teacher, the whole nine yards. But I don't want some man telling me I can't go to Florida because he says so. That I have to quit my job because he says so. That I have to be a replica of his mother because he says so," she said.

"You're right. It's complicated," he nodded. "Do you love him? Are you changing your mind?"

"I don't think I do love him or even did and I'm not changing my mind. It's history," she said.

A crowd of teenagers shoved their way through the front door, laughing, shoving, pointing to the humorous prepainted shirts decorating all the walls in the shop. A dozen or more of them all sporting shirts that declared they were from some church in Prosper, Texas.

"Can I help you?" she asked.

"We're just making up our minds about what we want," a pretty teenage girl with a long blond ponytail said. "We're going home tomorrow morning and we haven't bought a shirt yet."

"What if we want one out of this book?" A dark-haired young man asked.

"I'm afraid we'd have to mail it to you. We've got orders that will take most of the afternoon and maybe even part of tomorrow ahead of you. I'd be glad to take names and addresses if you want them mailed," she said.

"Oh, no! We want to wear them home. Shut that book, Tommy. We're not going to wait a week after we get home for a shirt," the girl shoved the boy looking at the book.

"I want this one," another teenager picked one off the wall and laid it beside the cash register. "If we hurry, we can still get a few hours of sun before the day ends."

"This one is mine," the girl said. "Tommy, let's go play miniature golf until curfew."

"Yes, darlin' Jodie," he grinned.

Twenty minutes later she'd rung up another thirteen sales. She'd have liked to visit more with Boone, try to explain even more what she was trying to get across to him. But suddenly she wondered why she wanted him to understand anyway. They'd only built a castle together and played pretend one time. That didn't warrant instant friendship. She looked out across the street at the sunbathers stretched out on towels and blankets, coolers beside them, books laid aside, portable CD players blaring, and she thought of the kids who'd just bought shirts. Darlin' Jodie would be playing golf with Tommy by now. Jodie had better enjoy all the teenage adoration.

"Boone, darling!" A tall blond woman, looking as if she'd just stepped off a model runway, swept into the shop, ignoring Dixie altogether as she focused on the man with the air brush in his hand.

"Anita, what are you doing in Florida?" His face registered pure shock.

Dixie crossed her arms over her chest and leaned back against the bar. If those walking shorts didn't come with a hundred dollar price tag and that shirt at least twice as much, she'd have a dirt sandwich for supper. The sandals looked like pure Italian leather. Anita pushed open the swinging door into Boone's private haven and wrapped her arms around his neck, grabbing a handful of blond hair and forcing his face down for a kiss that would have fogged the windows of a brothel.

"I've come to let you forgive me," she said in a

breathless tone, coming up for air only long enough to tell him that and then pull him back for another kiss.

Dixie should have turned her back and given them some privacy, but she couldn't. Not any more than she could have blinked. A bit of jealousy flared up from her heart and turned her a faint shade of chartreuse. She argued with herself, telling her envious streak that she had no right to begrudge Boone such a gorgeous lady. After all, maybe they'd built a real castle together, one where she was the queen and he was the handsome king and they would live happily ever after.

"Stop it, Anita!" Boone pushed her away.

Holy mother, was that a blush creeping up his neck? Dixie wondered as she continued to rudely watch the scenario unfold before her eyes like a television soap opera.

"Oh, honey, you know you love me. You certainly said it often enough that you convinced me anyway. Now it's time for you to come on home and get out of this sweatshop factory. I'm sorry I was so tacky. We'll plan a Christmas wedding like you wanted. Daddy will give us a honeymoon in France for two weeks instead of a long, long vacation. You can quit your job at the ju-co and come to work for Daddy in the oil business. He can always use someone as smart as you, and you'll never have to work in this horrid little shop again," she wrapped her arms around his waist and laid her head on his chest.

"Anita, it's over," Boone said.

Lines from the Sara Evans song filtered through

Dixie's mind. So Anita and Todd had been shaken out of the same tree and that kind of bossy attitude wasn't restricted to the male gender. Anita was the knight-in-shining armor and Boone was Cinderfella in the story. She'd rescue him from the squalid Ocean View T-shirt shop and they'd fly off on a magic chunk of Berber carpet to live happily ever after.

"Yes, I'm sure it was but now it's not. I've changed my mind," she said.

"I haven't. I'm going to teach until I retire probably right there at the same school because that's what I like to do. I come here because I love Florida and I paint T-shirts because that's what I want to do," he said.

"I'm offering you the deal of a lifetime," she told him. "And you can stop staring at us." She pointed a long, perfectly manicured finger at Dixie. "Don't they teach you anything down here in Florida about manners? This is a private conversation."

"Don't you be rude to her," Boone said.

"Oh, is this your summer plaything?" Anita turned on him, hatred and tension filling the air.

"No, this isn't my summer plaything," Boone smiled brightly but Dixie noticed it didn't reach his eyes. "This is my wife. Dixie, meet an old friend, Anita. Sorry about the kiss, darlin'. Please don't do anything voodoo like make Anita gain fifty pounds or give her chicken pox."

"Oh, honey, I wouldn't be that gentle," Dixie drew her eyebrows down in a frown and tried to think up one of Faith's many curses. "I was thinking more like making her poor and giving her a job painting T-shirts for a living."

"You really married someone like that?" Anita stared at Dixie.

"A week ago. We tied the knot right on the beach. In our bare feet. I wore shorts and an Ocean View T-shirt and she wore a bathing suit. Original, huh? We've only known each other two weeks. I thought she was a shoplifter the first time I met her." Boone stepped around Anita and went to the front of the store to slip his arm around Dixie's slim waist.

"You are disgusting," Anita stomped across the wooden floor, every angry step resounding through the whole shop. "I hope you regret this for the rest of your life. I hope you wake up every morning and look at Miss Plain-Jane and remember what you could have had. I hope you—"

"You've made your point, Anita. I hope you find a man who takes your breath away and makes you as happy as Boone and I are." Dixie snuggled in close to Boone's side, hamming up the part so well that Anita should have seen through it if she'd had a lick of common sense.

"Oh, I will honey, and he'll be twice the man Boone Callahan is," Anita snapped, stopping beside the cash register.

"There ain't a man out there that wonderful," Dixie said.

Anita disappeared without another word.

"Oh, really?" Boone looked down into Dixie's green eyes.

"You must learn to never take anything said in a cat fight seriously," Dixie slipped out of his arms. "That, kind sir slash employer slash husband slash stable boy will cost you double wages. So you'd better get on back in there and make more T-shirts."

"Thanks for playing along with me, Dixie. I didn't know how to make her leave and the idea was out of my mouth before I could even think. I had no idea she'd come to Florida. We haven't talked since March," Boone said seriously. "We parted company during spring break. It was a really nasty break up. I wanted her to marry me and move into my house in San Antonio. She wanted me to sell my house, quit teaching, take a year off to tour the world and settle down to work for her father in Houston. I really did think I loved her in spite of her money but . . . hey, I think this is your story turned around. I understand what you were talking about, now. Anita and Todd are just alike. Think we should introduce them?"

"Lord, no. They'd kill each other. With all that power they'd blow Arkansas right off the map in less than a week," Dixie said. "And you are welcome. If Todd ever comes waltzing in here like she did, I'll collect on the favor."

"Anytime. But let's see, the whole incident lasted about ten minutes. That would be double wages for one sixth of one hour. Think if I bought you a hot dog for supper it would cover the bill?" he asked mischievously.

"Hmmm," Dixie shut her eyes, as if deep in thought. "With chili and onions and cheese on top. A foot long at that. Yes, I think that would be an agreeable rate."

"A foot long! It was only ten minutes," Boone was already back in his part of the store when she opened her eyes.

"With an extra large root beer. Wives are expensive merchandise and I'm high maintenance," she laughed.

"A foot-long then and an extra large root beer and you'll sign the divorce papers?" he asked.

"Oh, no, honey, when I'm a wife, it's for eternity. Your impetuosness has you strapped to a Miss Plain Jane forever and ever," she teased right back.

"I certainly wouldn't call you Plain Jane, Dixie. And, honey, you sure didn't get much, either. A ju-co professor who is a beach bum all summer," he said.

"Some days it just don't pay to get out of bed," she said just before an older couple came wandering in off the sidewalk to shop for their grandchildren.

The sun was setting over the water, providing the last scene of a magnificent show for Dixie as she opened the door to the beach house that evening. She flipped on the light in the living room and kicked off her sandals. In the kitchen she unloaded her open weave beach bag. Half-eaten ham sandwich tossed in the trash. Two full bottles of water back in the refrigerator.

Chewing up two antacid pills to combat the chili and onions she'd had on the hot dog, she thought about the incident with Anita. She and Boone physically matched each other so well. Dixie poured a glass of milk and leaned on the counter, shutting her eyes. The vision of Anita floating down the aisle in a designer wedding dress of white bridal satin, a fluffy veil in all that blond hair and a ring with a diamond the size of a goose egg on her left hand was so real that Dixie could actually smell her expensive perfume. Boone waiting at the front of the church in a western-cut tux and a smile on his handsome face as he watched Anita coming closer and closer. The two of them leaving in a long white limo going toward a private leer jet.

The back door rattled, jerking Dixie back into reality with a start. She jumped, opened her eyes wide, trying to adjust from darkness to bright light and figure out who was in the house all at the same time.

"Jill?" she called out.

"No, it's Faith," she and a tall, lanky man appeared from the darkness into the light of the kitchen.

"Ahem," a man cleared his throat not two feet from her. He pushed his gold rimmed glasses back up on his nose. "You must be Dixie."

"Are you Jackson?" Dixie asked.

"I'm sorry," Faith said. "Dixie this is Jackson and Jackson, this is Dixie. I forgot you haven't met each other. We were just on our way to sit on the beach. Think I wouldn't scare the clams so bad they'd start digging their way to China?" she asked Dixie.

"I'm glad to finally meet you. I'd begun to think that you and Jill were just figments of Faith's imagination," he extended a hand.

Dixie shook it. The man didn't even look twenty-six. Any bartender in the whole state would make him produce an ID before they'd sell him a single beer. Granted he was pretty, even with the glasses. Blond hair. Blue eyes. An angular face that wouldn't need shaving more than twice a week. Totally unlike Boone's heavy beard.

"I'm glad to finally meet you, Jackson. And I don't think you'll frighten the fish anymore, Faith. Want a glass of tea? I'm about to pour myself one," Dixie said.

"Not me. I'm going to put on my bikini and pretend my skin is beautiful again," Faith disappeared into the bedroom.

"I'd love one. I'm so thirsty today. Must be the heat," Jackson smiled, his dimples deepening.

Dixie really looked at him. "Jackson, have you had chicken pox?" she asked.

"Sure. I must have had them when I was a child. I called home when Faith came down with them and Dad said he thought I'd had them. All kids get them when they're in grade school, don't they?" He took the tea from her and downed half the glass.

"Faith didn't," Dixie said, taking a step closer. "Raise up your shirt."

"Hey, Faith wouldn't want her friend hitting on me," he chuckled and blushed at the same time.

"Honey, I'm not hitting on you. There are four bumps on your forehead. I think you are a little old for pimples. Chicken pox start with a low grade fever and you just said you were thirsty. You look a little flushed. They also like to gather up around the tummy area first, so hike up that shirt, Mister, and let me check," Dixie said.

He pulled up his shirt and moaned when he saw all the bumps setting up house keeping on his body. "Oh, no, now it's ten days for me, too?"

"Afraid so, honey," she said. "Faith is just about over hers, so now she can return the favor and keep you company for the next ten days."

"We were going to sneak away to San Antonio. Fly over for a few days to celebrate hers being gone. Do the Alamo, the river walk, eat at La Margarita's." He plopped down on the sofa and threw his head back, shutting his eyes.

One thing for sure, they were both dramatic as the devil, Dixie thought. No wonder they got along so well . . . birds of a feather had flocked together. Monied. Beautiful. Dramatic.

"I don't think San Antonio would be very grateful if you infected the tourist trade with chicken pox," Dixie said.

"Probably not. Guess it's back to checkers and old movies," he sighed.

"Are you really twenty-six?" Dixie asked bluntly, sitting down in a rocking chair and pulling her tired legs up under her.

"As of last month. I don't really look my age, I know. But then neither does Faith," Jackson raised his head up and picked up his tea glass again. "These things really do itch. Faith kept fussing about it but I didn't believe her."

"You don't think Faith looks her age? And don't scratch. I'll wrap your hands in pillowcases if you don't keep them away from the bumps," Dixie threatened.

"No, Faith does not look thirty-five," Jackson said.

"She told you how old she is?" Dixie asked, amazed. She and Jill had to practically prick their fingers and sign affidavits in blood stating they'd never tell anyone Faith's true age. She lied by five years to most people and even at that, no one would believe she was a day over twenty-one.

"No, she didn't. And don't you dare tell her I know, either. I happened to see her driver's license one day when she was showing me a picture in her wallet. I don't care how old she is, Dixie. She could be forty and I'd still like her. She's more alive and vibrant, even with chicken pox, than any woman I've ever met. We clicked from the first minute we met," he said.

"Okay," Dixie said slowly. "But she'd like to know that."

"No, I don't want her to know that I know," Jackson started to scratch his forehead but quit when Dixie shook her head at him.

"So you like her?" Dixie asked.

"Yes, more than I've ever liked anyone. I never thought the nerd of Marion, Virginia, would ever find anyone like Faith," he grinned again.

"Ready? I'll get a couple bottles of water and a bag of chips. What's the matter? Did I miss something." Faith stopped in the middle of the floor to take in the scenario. Dixie was standing too close to Jackson, who was blushing.

"Jackson has chicken pox. I made him pull up his shirt and they're all over his midriff. There're four on his forehead," Dixie said.

"Is there anymore of that stuff to put in the bath water around here? I'd like to borrow it if there is," Jackson asked.

"Oh, you poor baby," Faith dropped her beach bag and rushed to hug him. "I'll take care of you. They only last ten days and then we'll go celebrate both of us conquering the enemy."

"Yes, we've got at least half a box in the bathroom cabinet," Dixie said. "You're welcome to it. Faith quit using it a couple of days ago."

"Twenty-sixty-year-old men aren't supposed to get chicken pox," he said woefully. "It's more than a little bit ego deflating, isn't it?"

"Did you go to private school, too?" Dixie asked.

"No, went to public school my whole life. Mother would have probably remembered for sure if I'd had them, but she's been dead for several years. Dad wasn't around much when I was growing up and of course, my stepmother wouldn't know anything about that time of my life. Besides it wouldn't matter anyway. I'd already kissed Faith by the time she realized she had chicken pox and not an allergic reaction to something we ate on that short cruise," he said.

"Just wondered. I thought maybe people who went to private school never caught anything like measles or chicken pox," she said.

"Evidently some of us escape it in public school, too. Ten more days in the house! Guess if we can stand each other's exclusive company for three weeks we'll pass the test of amorous endurance," he kissed Faith on the forehead.

"Spoken like a true knight in chicken pox armor," Dixie said.

"It's not a teasing matter," Faith declared seriously,

dragging Jackson out the back door, only to pop her head back in within a minute to wink wickedly at Dixie. "I've got him all to myself for another ten days. The voodoo gods have smiled upon me!"

Dixie gave her the thumbs up sign, picked up the remote and turned on the television. Anything to take her mind off Boone Callahan and his old flame. She surfed through the channels until she found an old rerun of *Friends*. The episode where Chandler proposed to Monica. That's what she wanted. Someone who loved her like that. All the candles. The man down on one knee with a ring in a velvet box. It didn't have to be a big diamond. It could even be so small that the naked eye would need a magnifying glass to find it. She wanted to hear the old worn-out words about how her love completed his life. She wanted that breathless feeling inside her chest, telling her that she'd found her soul mate. She wanted that blasted biological clock to stop ticking loudly in her heart.

"That's not too much to ask, is it?" she asked.

No one answered.

Chapter Seven

The bride stared at the lovely dress and headpiece hanging on the armoire. Tomorrow her father's dream would come true and the worst nightmare of her life would begin. The door into her bedroom creaked as it opened. She didn't even look to see who would be entering her private quarters at that time of night. After all, only the woman her father had hired to bring her food and attend to her needs was allowed through the armed guards, six men deep in the hallway outside the tower doors. There was no escape. She would marry the Duke at daybreak. The only other option was jumping out the window to her death on the stones below. Compared to marrying that horrible man who only wanted to marry her so she would produce an heir for him, death had begun to look good.

"Hello," a deep voice said right above Dixie.

She laid the book on her stomach and shielded her eyes with the back of her hand.

"I'm Vance Matthews. I'm chaperoning a bunch of young boys over in the house next door to yours for the next week. Want to join us in volleyball?" he asked.

"I don't think so. I've left this heroine in a precarious predicament," she motioned toward her book.

"Ah, a steamy romance," he laughed.

"That's right," Dixie said, rolling over on her stomach and finding her place.

"Pastor Vance! We've chosen teams and we're ready," a young boy yelled, his voice breaking somewhere in the middle of the sentence.

"See you around," Vance laughed.

"Oh, my lord, a preacher and a bunch of choir boys. Wait until I tell Faith. She'll be throwing Jackson back in the water and going fishing for something younger," she mumbled as she began to read again. Not four words later, the volleyball landed right in front of her, showering her book with sand.

Pastor Vance's face came mere inches from hers when he bent down to pick up the ball. Dark hair fell down over his forehead. Brown eyes twinkled in an angular face, not totally unlike the one on the front of her romance book. Take off the T-shirt and dress him in a pair of tight fitting trousers with some kind of tunic over his torso and he could be the Irishman in the story.

"Pardon us," he smiled, showing off even white teeth.

"Need a scorekeeper?" she asked, laying the book

aside. She'd never be able to keep her mind on it with a bunch of screaming boys so close by.

"Would love one," he nodded. "How much do you charge?"

"What are you serving for lunch?" she asked.

"Grilled hamburgers on the back porch," he told her.

"Then my fee is two burgers and a cold soda." She pulled the oversized T-shirt over her bathing suit and took the ball from his hands.

"Hey, guys, this is our new scorekeeper and ref," Vance yelled above the din at the boys on both sides of the net.

"Hi fellows. I'm Dixie Nelson from up in Greenbrier, Arkansas," she introduced herself. "I teach English at the high school there."

"Ah, man, does that mean we ain't supposed to say *ain't*?" One skinny kid asked.

"That's what it means," Vance said. "Now let's play ball."

Two hours later, the skinny kid's team had won four out of five games, and true to his word, Pastor Vance had donned a big apron over his T-shirt and swim trunks and was cooking hamburgers.

"Good Lord . . . oops . . . pardon me . . ." Dixie stammered. "Why are you cooking so many burgers? You're not feeding an army."

"Ten boys, age twelve, thirteen and one fourteen-year-old. All with a bigger appetite than Goliath, I'm sure," he smiled. "So Dixie, the boys are going to a movie tonight. They are good kids and I can trust them on their own for a couple of hours. Would you wander up and down the strip with me for a couple of hours?"

"But you are a . . ." she stumbled over the words again.

"I'm a pastor, not a priest," he told her. "In our faith we get to date beautiful women. We get to even kiss them. Our women don't even have to wear veils to cover their faces and last week one of them even bought a bikini. Of course, the older women in the congregation were jealous."

She laughed. "I'd love to stroll around with you for a couple of hours, Pastor Vance."

"Just Vance, please. The boys call me that because it's what their mothers tell them is proper and respectful. But please, just Vance for you. Hey, guys, dinner is served," he called inside the house. Games and a movie got put on hold while the boys consumed every bit of food in sight.

That evening she dressed in a bright colored gauzy skirt that swept around her ankles, an orange tank top and matching sandals. When she came out of the bedroom, Faith and Jackson both looked up from the sofa and Jill whistled through her teeth.

"So where are you going? Did you finally get Boone to ask you out? Are you going to take him home?" Faith fired questions so fast that Dixie scarcely had time to register them all.

"No, she's got a strolling around date with a preacher," Jill said from the other side of the room.

"A preacher!" Faith threw her head back and gazed

at the ceiling. "A preacher! First a sugar daddy and now a preacher. Are you going to come home saved, sanctified and dehorned?"

"Want me to keep my mouth shut?" Dixie stared at Jackson who was busy watching the evening news.

"I'll be good," Faith giggled.

"Come on Dixie, I can't see you giving up something that looks like Boone Callahan for a preacher. Somehow I can't picture you sitting on the front pew of church three or four times a week and being all that good." The corners of Jill's mouth twitched as she fought back a grin.

"I didn't say I was going to marry the man and I'm not giving up Boone. For one thing you have to have something in the first place in order to give it up, and I've never had Boone. And most likely never will. He's not ready for any rebound experience any more than I am. That witch he wanted to marry makes Todd look like Prince Charmin'," Dixie said. "I'm just taking a nice long walk with the pastor while his choir boys or altar boys or Sunday school class—whatever they're called—take in a movie. He's not a knight in shining armor, just a stable boy."

"Uh, oh," Jill intoned. "It's the stable boy who always upends the whole story and winds up with the princess."

"Is Dixie the princess in this castle?" Jackson looked up when the news ended. "I thought Faith was the princess."

"That's so sweet," Faith kissed him on the cheek.

The doorbell rang and Dixie shot them all a mean

look before she opened it. "Hello, Vance, come in and meet my friends."

"Just a minute. I've left the boys in the van and you know boys," he left the door open so his charges would know to keep the noise to a dull roar.

"This is Jill and this is Faith and her friend, Jackson," Dixie made introductions.

"It's not leprosy," Jackson stood and shook hands with Vance. "Chicken pox. The last stages, thank goodness. Faith had them first and then it was my turn."

Vance chuckled. "I'm glad it isn't anything worse. At least now you're immune for the rest of your life."

"Praise the Lord!" Faith exclaimed then blushed.

"I shall take that as a sincere praise and not blasphemy," Vance said.

"Thank you, Father," Faith dropped her head and covered her face with her hands.

"I'm not Father Vance. I'm Pastor Vance. Like I told Dixie, we are so modern that our pastors can marry and have families. We can even watch movies and have a glass of wine with supper."

"Oh, my," Faith said. "That's wonderful."

"Ready?" Vance offered Dixie his arm. "And it was nice to meet all of you. Maybe we'll get together for a cookout before we leave since we're next door neighbors for five more days."

"Not if I can help it," Faith said when they were out of the house. "I didn't come to Florida to spend even one night with a bunch of sweaty boys."

"Faith!" Jill chided.

"Not a bunch of sweaty boys, just one sweaty

chicken-pox-infected boy named Jackson Smith," Jackson teased. "Not to worry my princess Faith. We are booked for a flight to an island where our every whim will be catered to. Tomorrow morning at eight o'clock the charter will pick us up and take us away to paradise until Saturday morning."

"You'll have to entertain the sweaty little boys all alone, Jill. What a pity when I'd so looked forward to listening to seventh grade humor until the wee hours of the morning," Faith smiled at Jill.

"And that's pretty close to blasphemy," Jill shook her finger at Faith. "Actually I'm off on Wednesday to Mobile. I'm staying over until Saturday. Uncle Vincent has a benefit on Friday. Paul and I are going to dinner Thursday and spending Saturday together, then he's bringing me home on Saturday evening," Jill said.

"So we finally hear his name from your lips. Dixie and I've been calling him Mr. Rich," Faith told Jackson. "Want to share any more about your new flame?"

"No, but I thought if everyone was around we might have a beach party on Saturday night and let me introduce you to him. You can form your own opinions then. I'll tell Dixie later. She might want to bring her preacher."

"I'd rather she brought Boone," Faith said. "Preacher Pastor Vance isn't hard on the eyes. Mighty fine looking. But there's something weird about Dixie and a preacher."

"There is, isn't there? But at least he's not Todd Riley so maybe we'd better keep our opinions to ourselves," Jill said.

"Nope. According to the new rules of the PMS, honesty is the order of the day. And I say it's weird," Faith said.

"Then we'll tell Dixie it's weird if she wants to bring him and his passle of pimple faced boys. But if she says she's all tingly when he kisses her then we will respect that and learn to live with the weirdness," Jill said.

"Deal," Faith said.

"So do you get all tingly when I kiss you and does Dixie think I'm weird?" Jackson asked.

"Of course I get all tingly and no, Dixie does not think you are weird," Faith said.

"Is it going to be weird when Jill brings Paul home?" Jackson pulled Faith closer to his side, nuzzling the side of her neck.

"Of course not. Paul isn't a preacher or doesn't use a walking cane, does he?" Faith asked Jill.

"Neither one. He's not the hunk that Boone is but he's not ready for the rocking chair. He's a very nice man and I'm thinking about taking him home," Jill said.

"Then we'll have a party on the beach. I know a wonderful catering company who does a smash up job of a luau. I'll call tomorrow and make arrangements for them to take care of the party for us on Saturday," Jackson said.

"That's really nice. Thank you," Jill told him.

"You are very, very welcome. Now, tell me, what is this about taking stuff or people home?" Jackson asked.

"It's a PMS Club secret, sugar. You wouldn't be a bit interested in something a bunch of women talk about. Now, let's go watch the sun set over the ocean and see if I'm all tingly when you kiss me," Faith pulled him up off the sofa and dragged him out the back door.

Vance paid for the movie tickets and made sure all the boys were inside the theater before he and Dixie started walking down the strip. He reached down and took her hand in his and although no sparks flew up to create a fireworks show for the whole area, she didn't jerk it away. It really wasn't so strange, her hand tucked inside the pastor's.

"So where do you and this crew of boys live?" she asked.

"We're from Southaven, Mississippi. Little town just south of Memphis. One of the members of our congregation owns the beach house. After that last round of hurricanes, it had to have lots of repairs done. We gathered up every able-bodied man and boy in the church and spent a week down here working. They give us the use of it four weeks every summer and it seemed only fitting that we help them out. The boys and I come one week. The girls come another. Then the young married folks take a week, and the last one is for the older married couples fellowship retreat," he explained.

"Want to play miniature golf?" she asked.

"I'd rather just walk and visit. There's not much chance for adult conversation during this week. Especially with an intelligent, beautiful woman," Vance said.

"Then that's what we'll do," Dixie said. "What made you go into preaching?"

"Felt the call and couldn't run from it. Tried but God was very persistent," he said.

"Ever been married?" she asked.

"No, the church frowns on divorced pastors. Haven't found the right woman. Want to apply for the job?" he squeezed her hand.

"Bet you tell all the women they're beautiful and give them applications," she smiled up at him.

"Only the ones who truly are, and I have a very limited supply of applications," he teased. "The boys thought I should sweep you off your feet in one night. They said no one else knew nearly as much about volleyball as you. That you were a fair ref and kept score just right. They even said something about your pretty eyes and figure."

"Oh, and what does Pastor Vance think of my eyes and figure?" she asked.

"He thinks God made you very well," Vance said. "Oh, here's the shop I plan on taking the boys to on the last day so they can get a shirt to wear home. Come on. Let's go see what the artist is doing this year." He opened the door to the Ocean View T-shirt shop without letting go of her hand.

"So just where is your sweet little voodoo queen of a wife tonight?" Anita had her hands across her chest, tapping her foot on the wooden floor, her back to the front door. "I called your sister-in-law, Cara Ann, last night, Boone Callahan, and she told me you hadn't told the family one thing about getting married. I think you were lying to me."

"I was saving that as a surprise for when they all

come down here in August. Now you've spoiled it,"
Boone lied. He looked up to see who was coming
inside the shop and could have kissed Dixie right on the
spot. Her timing couldn't have been better but who was
the man with her? The one with her hand tucked so
tightly into his and "that look" in his eyes like he owned
Dixie. Holy smoke, had her Todd come back and she
was there to tell him she was quitting her job and running off to France for a honeymoon. His heart turned to
a lump of stone in his chest.

"Hi, Anita. So did I hear right, did you really call
Boone's family and tell them we were married?" Dixie
slipped into the wife role when she left Vance's side
and hugged up next to Boone, slipping her arm around
his waist. He must have truly put in a day because a
mixture of paint, sweat and faint aftershave clung to his
tense body.

"Yes, I did, and I don't believe you for a minute.
You're just saying that to hurt me because I hurt you,
aren't you?" She ignored Dixie and glared at Boone.

"Well, believe it sugar," Dixie said, honey covered
ice dripping from her tone.

"What?" Vance frowned. She'd not said a word about
being married. Hadn't even taken her hand from his all
the way down the street. She'd flirted almost as much
as he had all day.

"Who is this?" Anita turned to stare at Vance.

"My brother. He's here visiting and he's very happy
for us, aren't you, Vance? He's the preacher who married us on the beach so you wouldn't be disputing his
word, now would you, Anita? For goodness sake,

woman, Boone has told you he's not interested. You are shaming yourself with all this carryin' on," Dixie put on her best southern tone.

"Oh, I won't be embarrassing myself anymore," Anita said. "But you remember when he calls out for me in his sleep that the likes of you can't hold a man like Boone Callahan. It takes more money and woman than you'll ever have or be to keep him happy."

"If I ever hear him whimperin' for you, sugar, I'll worry about it that day. So far I haven't heard anything like that," Dixie snuggled in closer to Boone's side. Lord Almighty, but the sparks were flying around like someone had lit a Fourth of July sparkler right there under their shirts. Dixie didn't know if it was attraction or if it was just a first-rate cat fight in progress, but she hadn't felt so alive in weeks, maybe months or years.

Anita slammed the door as she left without another word.

"Another cat fight I wouldn't understand?" Boone looked down at Dixie. "Thank goodness you dropped in. She's pretty adamant about letting me forgive her."

"Want to tell me what's going on here?" Vance asked coldly.

"Oh, I'm sorry, I just had to come to my boss' rescue. That was his former fiancée who will have him forgive her for breaking his heart or be damned. Forgive the cussin', Pastor Vance," Dixie giggled but didn't leave Boone's side.

"You work here? I thought you were a teacher from Arkansas?" He shook his head.

"I work here on Friday, Saturday and Sunday part-time. Boone is my employer. This is Vance Matthews. He and a bunch of his church boys are living next door to us for the next few days. I refereed a volleyball tournament this morning so he fed me hamburgers and now we're having a walk while the boys are at the movies," Dixie said.

Thick gray tension filled the shop. If Dixie had had a coffee cup she could have reached out and filled it with one swipe through the air. She was reminded of the neighbor's tomcats when they squared off with each other in her backyard. On this side was Vance, the solid black tomcat. And on this one, Boone, the yellow and white tomcat. Any moment now the caterwauling would begin. Only trouble was when the tomcats squared off for a fur flying, it was usually over a female cat or a bowl of leftover spaghetti.

"Nice to meet you," Vance said coolly. "Then you two aren't really married?"

"No, I just told Anita that on the spur of the moment to get her to leave me alone," Boone said just as icily.

"Then are you ready to continue on down the walk?" Vance asked Dixie.

"Sure. See you on Friday, Boone," Dixie said.

Vance grabbed her hand as they left the shop but the tenderness was gone. She jerked it free and stopped in front of the gift store next to the T-shirt shop. She sat down on a park bench in front of the building and nodded at the seat beside her. "Now what is your problem?" she asked bluntly.

"I don't like being in the middle of a big lie like

that," he sat but he kept a foot of space between them. "I felt foolish and used and I'm not your brother."

"I apologize for putting you there. It wasn't very nice but Boone and I had to improvise with what we had. Anita is a first-rate . . ." She struggled to keep from saying the real word in her heart, ". . . witch. And not a good one."

"I don't care what or who she is, Dixie. That was childish and uncalled for. That man should be adult enough to tell the woman he's not interested anymore and let it go at that," Vance told her.

"Have you ever been in a relationship where your heart was broken?" she asked.

"Not since fifth grade when Salley Kay Johnson told me she liked my best friend better than me," Vance said, his jaws working in anger as he gritted his teeth. What had been the icing on a wonderful day had just turned sour.

"Well, Boone loved that woman. Really loved her and wanted to marry her. But she's got money on the brain. To have her, he would have to give up his job and work for her father. Most likely give up his family and friends," she said.

"Forsaking all others and cleave only unto thy wife," he recited. "That is what men and women are supposed to do."

"Oh, really. Tell me something, Pastor Vance. When you run through your applications for a wife, what is it you'll be looking for, other than a physical attraction?" she asked.

"I don't usually discuss these things on a first date," he said.

"Then make this an unusual first date," she told him.

"I'll be looking for someone with a sweet spirit who will be a help to me in the ministry. Someone who will be content to stay at home and raise a family for me. Who'll have my supper on the table and keep a peaceful home for me and the children. Who'll fit in with the congregation and be a willing, eager hostess. Who'll teach my children right from wrong. And it won't hurt if she's easy on the eyes," he tried to tease the anger from his soul.

"What if she wants to work outside the home. Have a baby-sitter to keep the children? Maybe a house cleaner once a week?" she asked.

"Oh, no, that applicant's papers will be shredded. My wife is not going to work. That breeds too much independence," he shook his head.

"Vance Matthews, this was a lovely day. I enjoyed the volleyball games. I enjoyed the burgers and the boys. You are a very handsome, charming man, but the date is now over. I'll find my own way home," she said bluntly.

"Hey, I didn't ask you to marry me, Dixie. I just wanted some adult conversation, maybe a good night kiss, the anticipation of seeing you again. I'm sorry I was so riled at the situation we walked into." He put up his hands in defense.

"Sorry, Pastor Vance, it would be a waste of time on both our parts. No hard feelings and you really should have a kiss for your time," she took his face in her hands and softly kissed his lips. "Good luck on finding that sweet little wife who'll make your heart do double time. And have a wonderful vacation with the boys."

She was back in the Ocean View T-shirt shop before he could answer. He sighed and walked back toward the theater. The kiss had been pleasant but it hadn't rocked his heart the way it had been shaken before. Especially when Mattie O'Brien had kissed him. Perhaps it was God's way of telling him that Mattie really was the woman for him and he needed to stop looking for someone else.

"What are you doing back here?" Boone asked from the back of the store where he worked on a few free-lance shirts to hang back on the walls. "Date already over?"

"Yep, it is. Need someone to work 'til closing?" She picked up a broom and began the job of sweeping up the never-ending sand.

"Sure. Want a root beer? I just stocked the refrigerator and hey, you look really good in orange. That outfit is stunning. Was it too much for the preacher man? Or did you swear?" he asked. Mercy, but he was glad to see her. That little twinge of jealousy when he'd looked up and saw her with another man had chipped away at his heart until he was in a royal snit. When she walked back in the shop, the mood disappeared.

"Yes, I'd like a root beer. I'll get it myself. Thank you for the compliment. Guess I did swear but not in cuss words. I must be too picky this summer. Morgan and his money didn't appeal to me. The preacher and his piety didn't work, either," she said.

"What are you looking for?" Boone put down the airbrush and laid the shirt to one side to dry.

"I don't know but I've got a feeling it'll hit me right between the eyes when I find it. Is that the last one for the evening?" She nodded toward the shirt.

"No, got another hour before closing. Probably get four more done now that you're here to fend off any late customers. What will it take to hit you right between the eyes, anyway, Dixie?" he asked.

"Love. Pure old love. Not money. Not pretty words. Just love. I'm not so sure happy-ever-after is even out there anymore Boone. At least outside of a romance book, that is," she opened the door to the tiny kitchenette and found a root beer in the fridge.

"Well, give me a romance book, then," he said seriously. "I didn't know it was out there anywhere."

"I've got just the one for you," Dixie laughed, her heart lighter than it had been since she left work on Sunday. "It's about the maiden who is being forced to marry the Duke when she's in love with a commoner."

"Sounds like the lady in our castle," Boone said.

"It sure does," Dixie downed half the bottle of soda. "I'll tell you about it while you paint."

Chapter Eight

Faith braided her long blond hair into a single rope down the back to keep it out of her eyes when she and Jackson played in the water. She'd had four days of pure heaven on some island that was definitely not a tourist trap. The chicken pox were nothing more than slightly reddened dots in her tan and Jackson assured her no one would even notice with a figure like she had. She chose an electric blue bikini for the luau with a matching sheer skirt that tied around her waist. She didn't really look thirty-five, she rationalized as she stood in front of the floor-length mirror in her bedroom. *But you need to tell him,* her conscience chided. *Things are beginning to get more serious than you'd thought they would and you need to be honest.*

"Not tonight," she whispered, blowing her reflection a kiss. "Tonight is the perfect ending to a perfect week.

Nothing can go wrong tonight, I'll tell him next week, I promise."

Jill lay three bathing suits and two outfits on the bed. Paul had said he would be wearing shorts, sandals, and a casual shirt. He had told her that he didn't plan on getting in the water or doing the hula for Jill so he'd leave his Speedo and grass skirt at home. Jill smiled at the vision of him in a grass skirt acting silly. Not her reserved Paul. She rejected all the bathing suits and chose a long summer cotton sheath, slit up the sides, sleeveless. She slipped it over her head, letting it fall down past her hourglass figure, and looked at herself in the mirror attached to the back of the bedroom door. She needed something to dress it up. Rustling around in a tote bag full of costume jewelry, she came upon her periapt. Just the right piece, she decided as she brushed back her brown hair and fastened the necklace. It went with the jungle scene printed on the bottom of the dress.

"So what will the girls think of Paul?" she asked the woman in the mirror.

They'll love him and say he's just the one for me to take home, she answered silently with a wicked grin. *After all, there is nothing not to love about Paul. He's gentle, kind, wants everything in life that I want. Tonight will be perfect.*

In the third bedroom, Dixie jerked her most comfortable one-piece bathing suit from the drawer and covered it with the shirt she'd bought the first day at the T-shirt shop. The scene had begun to fade but then she'd worn the thing almost every day since she'd bought it. Wore it all day, washed it every evening. That did have a way of taking its toll on paint and fabric. She had no one to impress that night. Pastor Vance had ignored her since their disastrous date and he and his hoard of choir boys had left early that morning. The house next door was empty once again. She'd told Boone they were having a luau and he was welcome to stop by after work, but he'd said he was going to shut up shop and work a couple of extra hours to restock the walls.

So it would be Faith and Jackson, Jill and Mr. Rich Paul. It seemed fitting. She'd had Todd for a whole year and they'd listened to her stories of Todd this, Todd that, Todd said and Todd did. Now it was her turn to listen to them, and she surely didn't begrudge them a minute of it, either. Hopefully neither Jackson nor Paul would turn out to be the kind of selfish buzzard Todd Riley was. Dixie looked at herself in the mirror and shook her head. She deftly pulled her dark hair up in a ponytail, securing it with a plain rubber band.

"There now. Dixie is ready for the big luau. The fifth wheel for the evening. But then the fifth wheel's job is easy. It just has to stay in the trunk in case there's a flat on one of the other four. So I'll stay in the background. It'll be a perfect evening. What could go wrong, anyway? Both Faith and Jill have found their knights in shining armor. And all I do is run off every stable boy who comes near me," she said.

"Hey, hey," Faith said when the other bedroom doors opened at the same time and Dixie and Jill came out into the living room. "Dixie has dressed down for the occasion and Jill has dressed up. Boone must not be coming and Paul is."

"That's the size of it," Dixie said. "But let it go on record that I did invite him. Albeit at the midnight hour, but I did."

"Oh, Dixie, did you wait until you were leaving to even tell him about the luau even though you knew about it all week? He could've come as a friend, not a prospective boyfriend." Jill pointed a finger and frowned.

"Yep, that's what I did. I was leaving the store when I told him we were having supper on the beach. Listen you two, I had a whole year with Todd and you two stood beside me. While it was alive with excitement and when it died violently. I'm just the friend this summer. I don't need a fling," Dixie said. "But I do need to eat. I'm starving and Jackson said there's even a roasted pig."

"Everyone needs a fling," Faith whispered when Jackson knocked on the door and came in without being invited. "Hi sugar. I'm ready."

"I see that, and you are lovely," Jackson brushed a kiss across Faith's lips. "We'll meet the rest of you at the foot of the stairs. That's where I had them set up the tables. There's a fire started and the music will begin in ten minutes."

"Paul should be here any time and we'll be right down," Jill said nervously.

"You know, we've all been so busy running here and

there that we haven't had a Monday night gritch-fest all summer," Dixie said.

"We do need to get back on schedule and have our Monday nights, don't we? I miss them, too. Do you think I should change? Am I overdressed? Paul said he'd be in casual clothes so I didn't want to wear a bathing suit," Jill fussed with the dress.

"Yes, I do—think you are overdressed. Take off the sandals and go in your bare feet. Other than that, you're going to knock him dead and he's the only one you are trying to impress tonight, so stop worrying," Dixie said.

"Thank you. We'll talk to Faith about a good time for a girls' night out, or rather a girls' night in. We haven't even had time to really talk about these relationships we've been thrown into. Uncle Vincent has finally finished his charity benefits so I'm free now, but I can't begrudge him one of them. Dixie, I've never felt so alive in my whole life. And I met Paul through that sweet elderly man. If Faith ever wants to give him away, I'd gladly adopt him as my legal uncle," Jill said.

"We need a Monday night. How about day after tomorrow?" Dixie asked.

"Can't. Paul and I are going to Nashville for the rest of the week. We're leaving Monday morning, coming home Friday night. He's got business there but his evenings are free and I can do the tourist things. Country Music Hall of Fame. Ryman Auditorium. Hey, maybe I'll even run into Sara Evans and tell her that her song changed your life," Jill said.

"Maybe so. I hear a car in the driveway. That would have to be the illusive Mr. Paul since I'm the fifth wheel tonight. And even if Boone had planned on showing up, he'd be on foot, not driving," Dixie nodded toward the door at the same time the bell chimed.

Jill feathered her hair back with a brush of her hand and hurried across the room. "Hi, Paul," she raised her lips for a brief kiss. "Come in and meet my friend. The others are already on the beach. This is Dixie." She led him across the room by the hand.

"Hello, Dixie. So which one are you? The one who works at a shirt shop or the one who's in love with a young entrepreneur?" Paul asked.

"I'm the working woman. I'm glad to meet you," she nodded. The man wasn't tall. He wasn't breathtakingly handsome with his thinning brown hair but his eyes were just plumb sexy. Deep brown with heavy brows above them. If he hadn't shaved before he left Mobile he'd definitely have a five o'clock shadow. She could see where Jill would be quite taken with Mr. Rich Paul. Especially with that soft southern accent and all that charm oozing out every pore in his body.

"Likewise," Paul said. "So did I overdress for the luau?"

Dixie smiled. Yep, they'd been tossed out of the same mold. She'd be surprised if she wasn't looking at bridesmaid's dresses before the next summer, maybe even before Christmas.

"Of course not. It's a casual affair," Jill said. "Let's go on down to the party before they carve that pig without us."

"They'd better not. I've already laid claim to half the ham," Dixie set off at a brisk pace across the floor and out the back door. A graceful escape to give them time for a real kiss before they had to share their time with the rest of the crew, she figured.

"Aha, the lady arrives," Boone said from the end of the steps. "I was on my way up to see if the invitation was still good."

Dixie stopped on the third step and shook her head. Surely it was a mirage. "I thought you had to work."

"Does that mean I need to go back to my RV and eat a tuna salad sandwich? Did you invite a preacher or a millionaire in my place?" he asked.

"Neither, and you are quite welcome to stay. A man shouldn't eat tuna fish when there's roasted pig just waiting to be carved and pineapple salad and crab cakes. Oh my, oh my," she scanned the tables spread before her from a vantage point.

Boone held out his hand. "Then shall this stable boy help the princess down the stairs and to the ball of the season?"

"Of course," she placed her hand in his. "But you're not the stable boy tonight. You're the butler. The stable boy wouldn't have a tux like you're wearing."

"Aha, Lady Dixie likes me for my fancy duds," Boone grinned.

Faded shorts that used to be dark denim. A T-shirt done up in his shop no less than five years before. Much, much sexier than a tux, she thought as she let him lead her to the edge of the water where Faith and Jackson were coming back from a short swim.

"Faith, come and meet Boone," Dixie called into the dusk.

"So we finally get to meet the slave driver," Faith stopped a few feet from Boone and Dixie and let Jackson catch up. "I thought you had to work late. Dixie was shedding tears and slinging tissues around. It looked like a snowstorm. I'm glad you could see fit to leave the million dollar business and join us."

Boone had to chuckle. Dixie had said Faith was a witty Cajun.

"Faith!" Dixie exclaimed. "Remember I'm holding secrets."

"And if you tell them, I'll really tell everything I know," Faith told her.

"Oh, can me and Boone stay and listen to the mud-slinging?" Jackson asked.

"Hello, Jackson. Haven't seen you this summer," Boone extended a hand.

"Been busy with this queen of sass and the chicken pox," Jackson said. "But I'll be by before the summer's end. My wardrobe is in dire need of shirts to keep me going until you start up business again next year."

"You two know each other?" Faith asked.

"Sure. Boone is my tailor. Paints all my shirts. Both those I wear year round and the ones I use to promote new games," Jackson said.

"Small world," Faith muttered. "Hey, there's Jill and her feller. Let's go make ourselves acquainted."

Just short of the bottom of the steps, Faith stopped so quickly that Jackson was jerked backward when he didn't let go of her hand. Even in the flickering light of the pit fire, Dixie could see that her face had gone ashy white. For a moment, Dixie feared that she was about to faint.

"Hello, Travis," Faith said in a hoarse whisper. "What are you doing here?"

"Travis? You're seeing things," Jill giggled nervously. "Everyone, this is Paul Beauchamp. The man I've been talking about these past weeks. He's from over in New Orleans."

"Faith," Paul said tersely. "So you are the other friend Jill has talked about. The one who dates the young entrepreneur."

"What's going on here?" Dixie finally asked.

"Travis Paul Beauchamp," Faith said. "We knew each other a lifetime ago. I was just shocked to see him after all these years. No introductions needed for us. But this is Jackson Smith, my . . ."

"Hello, Jackson. Haven't seen you in all summer. You usually make at least one of the charity benefits," Paul said.

"Chicken pox. This hussy gave me chicken pox," Jackson said. "I contributed but I couldn't attend. Now let's fill up our plates and take them over to the fire. There's blankets to sit on and the fire is low enough to keep us from scorching."

"Travis?" Dixie whispered to Faith as they held their plates for the caterers to fill. "Not *the* Travis. The old ex-boyfriend."

"The very one," Faith said.

"This is too weird," Dixie said. "Jill will never . . ."

"Yes, she will," Faith hissed. "Don't you say a word if she doesn't make the connection."

"Is he your Travis?" Jill said so low only Dixie and Faith heard her.

"We'll talk about it later," Faith said.

"I'll tell him . . ." Jill said.

"Later!" Faith said. "Jackson, darlin', is that really pineapple salad?"

"Yes, I know how much you liked it in the islands so I called early this morning and put it on the menu for tonight. Now let's go find a spot and pretend we are in Hawaii," he said.

"Maybe we will be before the summer is over," she teased, but her voice held an edge that Dixie and Jill both heard.

"So how is it that you two already knew each other?" Jackson asked innocently when they were all sitting around the glowing embers of a pit fire.

"Travis, I mean Paul, and I go way back. Our families knew each other even before we were born. We were both raised in private schools but we saw each other through the summer months and holidays. We graduated the same year and attended the same college," Faith said.

"Oh?" Jackson's mouth twitched at the corners. She'd just told on herself and didn't even realize it. Later when they had the age difference conversation, he would remind her that she'd left a trail of hints.

"Yes, and then we dated for a few years. But we grew apart and Faith moved away. I guess to Arkansas since that's where Jill is from and she told me she and her two friends all taught in the same school system. Never thought Faith would stay with teaching, though. Figured she'd be off climbing a mountain, hang gliding or some other adventurous thing," Paul said.

"My kind of woman," Jackson forked a piece of ham from Faith's plate. "What do you say we go for a long walk before we have dessert," he said to Faith.

"My heart is broken," she leaned into his shoulder. "I thought I was dessert."

"Ah, my adventurous woman, you are. But man can not live on love alone. He must have chocolate cake and good espresso occasionally," Jackson teased, sensing the stress amongst the women. Something he'd never seen in the weeks he'd known them. They amused one another, stood up for one another, but never was there a bit of anxiety. Not until Paul came on the scene. He'd be willing to bet half his fortune that there had been more to the relationship than a few dates several years ago.

Faith crammed the last bit of salad in her mouth and nodded. "Then excuse us, folks. We'll be back shortly for dessert. Boone please don't make Dixie mad while I'm gone."

"What was that all about?" Boone felt the major part of the anxiety leave with Faith and Jackson. So there had been a problem between Faith and Paul. Dixie would have to fill him in on the details tomorrow.

"When Dixie gets mad she eats," Jill said nervously. What were the chances of her meeting and falling for Faith's ex. Six trillion to one and yet she had. She'd have to break it off if she meant to keep Faith's friendship. Talk about weird. Not even Dixie's aging million-aire or her preacher could beat this situation. She wished the evening would end so she could talk to Faith, but her heart ached at the thought of not seeing Paul again. Her soul was torn between love and friendship.

"Oh, really?" Boone looked at Dixie's plate, still half full.

"Yes, some women pout and some scream and talk an issue to death. Dixie eats her anger away," Jill told them.

"She must not have been mad very often or she'd be big as—" Boone stopped before he said an offensive word.

"As a hippo?" Dixie set her plate on the blanket and slapped his arm. "Way I figure it is that calories and fat grams have no value when a woman is fire engine mad. The rage breaks them all down and they disappear. Then the food feeds the anger and it becomes docile in return."

"Good thinking," Paul said, glad Faith had gone away for a while. Just how this would affect his relationship with Jill scared the bejesus right out of him. He really liked Jill. Loved being with her. Hated the idea that she might decide she couldn't see him again because of Faith. Damn it all anyway. Faith had run out on him. Hadn't wanted the same things he did evidently. Now she could ruin a good second chance at happiness. It wasn't fair.

"I think so," Dixie said. "Now Boone Callahan, how 'bout me and you . . ."

"The English teacher just spoke badly," Boone set his empty plate aside.

"Then how about you and I take a walk up the beach also, and give this couple a little while alone. He didn't drive all the way from Mobile to listen to my tales about calories and rage," Dixie said.

"My RV is half a mile down the beach. If I wasn't so full I'd race you," Boone said.

"If I had to die or run, they'd have to blindfold me and bring on the firing squad," Dixie told him.

"Okay, love, tell me about Travis Paul Beauchamp." Jackson said when they were several yards down the beach.

"He wanted to marry me. I kept putting it off with one excuse or the other. Finally I just flat broke it off. Then seemed like everytime I turned around, there he was, so I went to Arkansas and lost myself in teaching. My folks were careful not to tell anyone where I was even though they thought I'd lost my mind. I'd meet them somewhere for Christmas holidays and a couple of weeks in the summer. France. Sweden. England. Hawaii. Wherever. It's worked fine until now. Who would have ever thought Jill would meet him. I figured he got married and had a dozen kids by now," Faith said.

"What was it he wanted that you didn't?" Jackson asked.

"The family thing. I'd be a terrible mother, Jackson. I teach kids all day. I don't want to come home to them at night. I don't want the yard and the PTA and a big yellow dog. Does that sound crazy to you?" she asked.

"Not one bit," he drew her into his embrace and kissed her soundly. "PTA isn't for everyone, you know. And I'm terrified of big yellow dogs. Thanks for being honest with me, Faith."

Honest, her conscience screamed. *Now is the time for you to be really honest.*

But she simply leaned into his chest, enjoying the comfort there and ignored the yelling in her mind.

"Paul, I don't know what to say. I had no idea you were Faith's . . ." Jill said when they were alone.

"Does it really matter? That was a long time ago and in the past. I'm a different person now than I was then, Jill. It doesn't seem like Faith is, though. Had I known she was your friend, I wouldn't have come tonight. Not until you would have had time to discuss it with her, *cher.* But now it is out in the open. I don't suppose we'll have to spend all our time with her will we?" he asked.

"No, of course not," Jill said. "But she is my friend. She's been there for me for five long hard years, Paul. I can't toss that in the garbage. This is so complicated."

"Of course it is, sugar. Life is complicated. You talk to Faith and I'll call you tomorrow. For tonight, come here and let me hold you while we watch the moon rise and the ocean waves glide in and out. Let's just enjoy each other and not worry about the past or the future. This moment is all we have anyway and I'm content to share it with you, Jill Coleman," he drew her close enough that her head rested on his shoulder.

"That was more than a little tense back there," Boone said.

"All we've heard for five years is how rotten Travis is. We didn't even bother to ask his last name, but we had this man conjured up who was half-devil and half-werewolf. He was egotistical. Thought he could make Faith be the same kind of woman Todd wanted me to be. A showpiece, trophy kind of wife. Not a real person with ideas and opinions of her own. Now it turns out he's a nice man and Jill really likes him, and oh, my lord, but it's going to be strange," Dixie rambled.

"Why? Their relationship is finished. Has been for a long time from what I could gather. Faith has Jackson now. Why shouldn't Jill and Paul enjoy their relationship?" Boone asked.

"You are a man. You would think that way. Paul probably does, too. But we've been closer than sisters for five years. We've shared everything. Now Jill won't be able to share things about Paul or else Faith will get all catty. And if Jill and Paul were to ever get together permanently, then if he made her mad, Faith would tell her that she knew he was a loser. Don't you understand?" Dixie asked.

"No, afraid I don't," Boone said. "Want to sit awhile?"

"Sure," Dixie drew her sandals off and put her feet in the cool water. The water slapped against her thighs. She edged down a few more feet so it would splash up to her waist when it moved toward her.

"I'm over Anita and I don't care who she dates," Boone tried again to make sense of the crazy situation.

"How about if it was Crock?" Dixie asked.

"Crock is married already," Boone answered.

"But what if he wasn't. What if he showed up on the doorstep at Christmas with Anita on his arm and told everyone they were engaged?" Dixie asked.

"I'd put out a contract on the woman," Boone said bluntly. "She'd ruin Crock's life. She's not his type."

"Exactly. That's what Faith is thinking right now. But Jill is thinking something different altogether," Dixie said.

"But what has that got to do with Anita and Crock?" Boone asked. "I still can't make much sense of it."

"What if Anita and Crock hit if off beautifully? What if they fell in love? What if they were soul mates? If their hearts went together so perfectly the two were one without a single crack where they were joined?" Dixie asked.

"No way. She's pure poison. But I think I'm beginning to understand what you are saying," Boone said. "Women friends are sure different than guy friends, though."

"That's because you are from Mars and we are from Venus," Dixie told him in wide-eyed innocence.

"I read that book. Can't say as it made a bit of sense," Boone said.

"Of course not, darlin'. Little stable boys from Mars can't read between the lines," Dixie told him.

"Maybe not, but I do remember chocolate cake being mentioned back there and I reckon we've given every-one time to sort out the story so they can all be civil adults when we get back," Boone said.

"Chocolate cake would tame any beast," Dixie grabbed her shoes and started back toward the campfire.

"Even anger?" Boone asked, itching to touch her hand, but avoiding every contact with her. He might be over Anita and ready to look at another woman, but he wasn't ready to fill the place of just a rebound boyfriend.

"If there's enough of it," she laughed and took off in a jog.

Chapter Nine

Dixie opened the freezer and took out half a gallon of Rocky Road ice cream. She rustled around in the silverware drawer and found three clean spoons. She set the ice cream in the middle of the coffee table, opened it, shoving the cardboard lid to one side and stuck all three spoons in the hard ice cream. It looked somewhat like a dirt pile with three lightning rods sticking out of it.

"Okay, Monday is too far away. Things could fester that would never get healed up right if we wait another week to get this talked through. So tonight we talk, even if it is late. I declare this an open meeting of the Periapt Magnolia Sisterhood and I'll have the first bite of ice cream," Dixie dug deep and brought up a heaping spoonful, complete with marshmallows and nuts.

"I don't even know where to start," Jill picked up a spoon and followed suit.

"Me, either," Faith did the same.

"Then I'll start since I'm not in the hot water," Dixie said. "How are you feeling about this Faith?"

"I've been asking myself that all evening. I tried not to be a witch. Jackson didn't need his expensive luau spoiled," Faith said.

"Ah, the voodoo queen of Arkansas thinks of someone other than herself," Dixie filled her mouth with rich chocolate goo that far outdid the chocolate cake the luau people had brought.

"Of course I did. I care about Jackson. I sure wouldn't want to hurt his feelings. Now that rascal, Travis, he should have been thrown into a swamp for gator bait years ago and we wouldn't have this to contend with tonight," Faith said.

"Don't say that. He's not a rascal, Faith. I happen to care as much about him as you do Jackson. I tried to keep the evening light so he wouldn't melt under the weight of the tension," Jill said.

"Season eight of Friends," Dixie said.

"What's that got to do with anything?" Faith said.

"Remember when Joey fell in love with Rachel, when she was pregnant with Ross' baby? That was a lot more baggage than we have here tonight and those friends handled it," Dixie reminded them.

"Sure they did. They read the script perfectly. But this is a little deeper than that, Dixie," Jill told her.

"How?" Dixie asked.

"For starters, it's Travis Beauchamp," Faith said. "He's not right for Jill. He'll insist she be his trophy wife. Go to all the fancy functions and have his heir."

"What if that's what she wants?" Dixie asked.

"It isn't. None of us want that kind of life. We want our independence. We want to teach school and play in the summer," Faith said.

"Yes, it is," Jill said softly. "It is what I want. We never talked about the distant future did we? At all those Monday night gritch-fests we teased about our biological clocks ticking so loud we could hear them above the fire siren. We shared everything but what was the deepest secrets in our hearts. Some big fancy named club we were. Those friends in the real Ya-Ya's might have kept things from everyone else, but not one another. Well, let's do it right now. We know Faith doesn't want a family and that's fine. It's not going to change our friendship one bit. But I do want one, Faith. I want a baby so bad I could just curl up and die from it. Not only do I want one, I want a dozen if I've got time to have them all. And I wouldn't care if I never set foot in another classroom in my life. I can't imagine why, with all your money, and proposed hatred of kids that you teach. Why aren't you like Jackson? Running here and there, a week in France, two in Hawaii."

"Because teaching makes me feel needed," Faith's chin quivered. "I don't have to work. My trust fund won't ever run dry, but there's a deep need in my heart for someone to need me. If things were to work out with Jackson, I might be content to follow him all over the world and play because he would need me. But according to my psychoanalyst—don't look at me like that—all rich people have counseling. According to her, my parents were so busy with their own lives they didn't need me. And I have this driving desire for someone to need me."

"Exposed nerves are beginning to show," Dixie said. "But the thing right now is whether we can weather this Travis Paul thing. Can you live with knowing that down the road in the future, you'll have to see him with Jill? Reckon you could bear not saying, 'I told you so,' when they have their first big fight?"

"I don't know," Faith said. "I thought I could change him. Make him see that we were the special people. The ones with their pictures on tabloids and the front page of the rich and shameless."

"You left him," Jill pointed the spoon at her.

"Yes, I did. But I had to. He would have smothered me plumb to death, sugar. I would have been Mrs. Travis Paul Beauchamp in six months. I'd have never been Faith Galaway again. The marriage license would have been the same as her death certificate. I don't want that to happen to you, Jill. I want you to always be Jill Coleman," Faith said.

"I will be. I'm strong enough that no man is going to completely wipe me out of existence," Jill told her.

"He's just another Todd Riley," Faith said.

"No, I don't think he is," Dixie dipped into the ice cream.

"This isn't your fight," Faith's spoon clanked against hers.

"Sorry, darlin', but it is. Anything that chips away at the PMS Club is my fight, too. We'll have to get this settled before we go to bed so it's my fight, too," Dixie disagreed.

"Do you really, really like that slug?" Faith asked Jill. "Be honest."

"Yes, I do. And if you call him a slug again, I'll have to ask you out at dawn for a duel. Weapon of your choice," Jill said.

"See there. He's a slug to me. Pardon me, not to you. But to you he's past the frog stage and already transformed into the prince," Faith said.

"Well, Jackson is a flighty young man to me, and he's already past the tadpole stage and wearing a crown, too," Jill said.

"You really feel that way about Jackson?" Faith's eyes popped open wide.

"Time out. The moderator of this meeting says we'll each eat five bites of ice cream before we speak again," Dixie said.

Whew, Dixie thought as she very, very slowly ate her first bite of ice cream. The slower the better. Even if Jill and Faith both gulped theirs down and put their emotional boxing gloves on for the second round, they couldn't say a word until she'd eaten her five bites. And she fully well intended to stretch it out as long as possible. Could it be possible that one man was going to rip the PMS Club into shreds? Dixie didn't think so. They'd been through too much together, but it might sure enough take a beating.

"Can't you eat any faster?" Faith asked after fifteen minutes and Dixie was still licking a her fourth spoonful of ice cream.

"Five spoons," Dixie said. "Think while I'm eating. Not like a couple of high school cheerleaders but like the friends we are."

"Are you calling us immature high school cheerleaders?" Jill asked incredulously. To think she'd been entertaining notions of telling Paul she wouldn't see him again. Well, that wasn't going to happen.

"I'm saying that we are thirty-five years old and we can work this out. Do we need to get out the PMS Club picture book?" She caused them both to remember the album they'd started as a joke after they'd watched the Ya-Ya's the second time.

"What good would that do?" Jill asked.

"You think you could still be mad at each other if you looked at that book?" Dixie asked.

"No," Faith said.

"No," Jill echoed, a giggle escaping her lips when she thought about the first picture in the book, of the three of them in flower pot hats and no makeup.

"So how are we going to handle this?" Dixie stuck her spoon back in the ice cream.

"I'm not going to let it affect me. I'm going to be there for you if he's a skunk or if he's the sweetest man in the world," Faith said. "I won't judge and I won't dredge up all his past mistakes. It really was my fault that we didn't stay together. I wasn't ready for his lifestyle. He didn't need me to be happy, Jill. He didn't need anything or anyone back then. Maybe he needs you."

"And I'm sure Jackson needs you," Jill moved closer to give Faith a hug. "I was just lashing out and being a witch when I said that. I'm sorry."

"Are you going to take him home?" Faith asked.

"I don't know. I'm going to take lots of memories home for sure. And maybe it will work into something that is permanent. My clock is ticking, even without the batteries, pretty loudly. But I'm not in a hurry with this, Faith. I want to give it time. I hope it works. I don't think I've ever felt so alive in my whole life. Not even with my husband. We were friends who sort of fell into marriage. This is something I can't even explain," Jill said.

"I can in one word. Jackson," Faith said.

"Then you know what I'm talking about," Jill nodded.

"And I'm jealous as hell," Dixie said. "You come down here and find happiness in one word and I can't find it when it falls right in my lap. It's me who's been moaning for a year about a wedding, and I've pushed away two perfectly good prospects."

"Well, sugar, it would take more than half a gallon of Rocky Road for us to talk you out of a millionaire sugar daddy or a preacher man for that matter if you really wanted one of them," Faith giggled.

"Would you have tried?" Dixie asked.

"Oh, honey, we would have hog-tied you and kept you locked up in a Louisiana bayou swamp cabin before we'd seen you take up with either of those fellers on a permanent basis. A dinner at a fancy restaurant or a volleyball game, why that's just funnin' but if you'd gotten serious, we would have had a long, long talk," Faith told her.

"What if I think neither of those men are right for you?" Dixie's temper flared. How dare they think they could decide who she'd like or love.

"Temper, temper. We've only got half the ice cream left," Jill said. "We promised to be honest from now on, didn't we? We stood by and bit our tongues through the Todd Riley affair. The rules have been amended. So now you tell us just what's the matter with Paul Beauchamp?"

"He's a bunch too rich, a little too smooth, and you'll have to keep him on a short leash. With that southern accent and the way he says *cher,* he could charm the hair off a frog's butt. Every woman he comes into contact with will be a threat to you," Dixie said.

"I've got a short leash, and I reckon I can hold my own with any bar room rosie with dollar signs in her eyes," Jill laughed.

"And Jackson?" Faith asked.

"He's twenty-six, for crying out loud. When are you going to tell him you are thirty-five? He doesn't have a biological clock. He can play for years and years, then if he decides to make babies, he still can get the job done. He's a nice enough man, but he's rich enough and eccentric enough you'll have to keep a two-by-four beside the door to keep the women from melting all over him just to get at that money and his sweet little grin," Dixie said.

"I'm going to tell him next weekend. That's a promise. That eccentric part is why I like him so much. On the spur of the moment, he decides to take me to this island where I'm sure the original Garden of Eden was located. While we were there he got this idea for a game and while I read a big, sexy novel, he worked two days on developing it. By the time we got home, he'd made a million dollars with the thing," Faith said.

"And Boone Callahan?" Jill asked.

"What about Boone?" Dixie asked right back, almost too fast, high color flushing her cheeks.

"We've bared our souls to raw skin about Paul and Jackson. Now we want to know about Boone," Faith said.

"There's nothing to know. I work for him. He's an almost-friend. I covered his sorry rear end with his ex, Anita. I told you about that already. He gave me a root beer when things didn't work with Pastor Vance," Dixie said.

"She's in denial," Jill poked Faith's arm with her finger.

"Happens when a woman is on the rebound," Faith said. "The right man comes along and she *thinks* it's just a rebound thing. Lets him slip right through her fingers and out of her heart because she's too stupid to see a good thing when it's put at her feet. Men like Boone are not rebound material. They're the real stuff."

"You two are crazy. Jackson could be a rebound thing," Dixie retaliated.

"I hardly think so. Let's see," Faith rolled her pretty eyes toward the ceiling, "rebound would have been Harvey Singleton. Remember the girls' basketball coach the first year we were in Greenbrier. Now that would have been rebound."

"Harvey never was right for you," Dixie said.

"Right, but he was rebound. Boone ain't. He's handsome, close enough to get personal with, and just downright pretty," Faith told her.

"Boone wouldn't ever be interested in me. You

should've seen Anita. She was gorgeous. I mean runway model pretty. That's his type. Not me," Dixie said.

"We'll just have to see how the summer plays out won't we? Maybe Mr. Aging Millionaire or Pretty Preacher would have had a chance if the vision of Boone Callahan hadn't been lurking around in the background," Jill said.

"You both are sleep deprived, emotional wrecks from Venus right now," Dixie declared. "At best Boone will only be a friend. All I'll get to take home is a new T-shirt or a shell from the beach. But rest assured I do envy the both of you."

"Are we all settled? Can this meeting be adjourned?" Faith yawned and pointed toward the clock.

"Meeting adjourned," Dixie declared with a click of her dirty spoon against the coffee table. "Next meeting one week from Monday and every Monday thereafter. No more missed meetings even if we are living in paradise. The Periapt Magnolia Sisterhood meeting is officially over. Good night, you two. And I'm glad we got it all settled."

"Me too," Jill hugged Faith again.

"Do I really have to tell him next week? Can't it wait until the end of the summer? What if he sees me as an old woman and doesn't want to be seen with me again?" Faith moaned.

"Yes, you have to tell him," Dixie said. "He won't dump you, I promise."

"Oh, what do you know. You can't even see that

Boone has stars in his eyes every time he looks at you!"
Faith threw a pillow from the sofa at her.

Dixie threw it back then ran into her bedroom. She
smiled when the soft thump hit the door. They were
back on familiar ground. She peeled out of her T-shirt
and wet bathing suit and stepped into the bathroom. A
luxury deluxe. Each bedroom had its own very small
bathroom. A toilet, small vanity and tiny, little corner
shower. The big bathroom in the hallway held a garden
style tub and a vanity with three mirrors. Tonight Dixie
was just glad for a hot shower to pound the knotted up
muscles from her neck and shoulders.

So the girls thought Boone was going to be her take-
home beach pretty thing. She might like that given half
a chance, but she wasn't blind or stupid. She'd seen
Anita. And she'd seen the way Boone's eyes strayed to
the front when a tall, blond customer came inside the
shop.

When the water was barely lukewarm she turned it
off and rubbed one of the enormous white towels over
her body until there wasn't even one droplet of mois-
ture. She pulled on a pair of underpants. Not thongs.
The one time she'd tried them she wiggled and tried to
pick them out of her fanny all evening. That was her
first date with Todd. And she wasn't going to remember
him all summer. Not even bikinis. Second date with
Todd and she'd felt like her underpants were falling all
evening. She had to get him out of her mind. She
checked the reflection in the mirror—plain old granny
panties according to her mother. Plain old Dixie to go
with them. Tall, blond models wore thongs and bikinis.

She jerked a tank top that looked more like a man's gauze undershirt than a pajama top over the top of her semi-wet hair. Slipping between the cool, crisp sheets on her bed, she figured she'd be asleep before her head carved out a comfortable place on the pillow.

She was wrong.

An hour later when the sun slapped the darkness away, she was still staring at the ceiling, wondering what she would do if Boone did pay any attention to her.

Chapter Ten

Black clouds gathered out on the ocean. Sun rays fought their way through but they were barely winning a battle, certainly not the whole war. Usually crowded, the beach had only a few die-hards trying to catch a bit of sun. Even those had left by four o'clock. Business was slow so Boone worked on replenishing the ready-to-buy stock. Dixie had straightened, swept and watched the clouds for more than an hour when the sun finally lost its place and the first rain drops fell.

"Time to batten down the hatches," Boone turned the radio station from constant country music to the weather station.

". . . not to panic. This is a tropical storm but by no means a hurricane. Several inches of rain will fall and the temperature will drop drastically for today and

132

tomorrow. By Wednesday the sun will be back out and everything will be back to normal," the announcer said.

Boone left his post and began the job of shutting the open window beside the register. He pulled the flap down, secured it with a series of locks and bolts. Then he picked up the heavy cash register and lugged it to the back of the store.

"What can I do to help?" Dixie asked.

"Nothing, I just need to get everything off the floor," Boone had already started moving shirts from the bottom cubby holes, cramming them in with the ones on the top.

"I can do that," Dixie grimaced at the way he was poking them in wherever he could with no regard to order.

"You can go on home before the bad part hits," he said. "There won't be any customers wanting shirts in this kind of weather."

"Move over and let me help," she nudged him with a hip and went to work beside him.

"It'll be too late for you to get home in another ten or fifteen minutes, Dixie," he said without breaking stride.

Dixie didn't ever want to see this man clean house. She couldn't begin to imagine what his office looked like. Maybe he had a tall blond secretary who kept everything nice and neat for him. Anita's twin, with perfect red fingernails, lipstick that never sunk down in the little crevices around the mouth, short skirts and high heels.

"Get out or you'll be in until it's over and that could be hours," Boone kept shoving T-shirts.

". . . she's blown ashore at Pensacola. Winds topping sixty miles an hour with lots of rain. It's moving slow-ly so the folks in that area can expect rain to last all day. Apologies to all you sunbathers and vacationers," the weather forecaster attempted to make light of the situation.

"Too late," Boone said gruffly.

"Well I am so sorry that you have to put up with me all afternoon. I'll try to be quiet and not get in your way," she snapped right back.

"You do that," Boone said.

Dixie shot him a hateful look. It would take her all afternoon to get his mess cleaned up. "I'll finish up here. You go paint shirts and stay out of my way, too."

"Hey, who's the boss around here?" he said. He should have known better than to hire a prissy schoolteacher. She probably had special little colored folders with each student's name in some kind of fancy script in her file cabinets. He could imagine her planning book, printed so neatly that it looked like it had come off a typewriter.

"Don't you take that tone with me," she said.

"Or what? You'll send me to the principal's office?" he all but growled before he went back to his painting.

Dixie didn't figure that comment even warranted a witty comeback. Whatever had crawled up Boone Callahan's cute little butt was his problem, not hers. It didn't take one of Faith's psychoanalysts to figure out Boone had a woman problem. Money caused men to frown and scratch their heads. Women made them snap and bite like a mean old hound dog. So when had Anita been back in? She wondered.

Rain beating on the wooden flap as well as the door sounded like Arkansas hailstones. The roar of the wind obliterated the weatherman's announcements. But then they didn't need to hear what was going on in Pensacola, Florida. They were right there in the midst of it, experiencing the whole thing in a very up close and personal way. Up close in that it sounded like the T-shirt shop might be blown all the way to Greenbrier by the time the wind abated. Personal in that the tension in the shop outweighed the fiasco on the beach when Paul showed up. Dixie shook her head trying to erase the idea that she should have gone home when he suggested it. Suggest, be hanged—he had demanded. Not totally unlike Todd had demanded. That sure didn't earn him any bonus points for exemplary behavior. And Dixie Nelson wouldn't be told what to do. Not by Todd and certainly not by Boone, who wasn't anything but her employer.

Boone stretched a shirt with three X's on the tag over a board and began an ocean scene on it. One with dark clouds in the background, the sea oats waving in the wind, one lone beach lounge chair over to one side. The story of his life in a air brushed shirt. He was the lounge chair weathering the coming storm. The sea oats were what he wanted out of life, just blowing in the wind, about to be flattened when the storm reached shore.

He didn't want to like Dixie. He sure didn't want to fall for her, but somewhere in the last six weeks it had happened, and he wasn't going to accept it without a full fledged fight. She wasn't his type. The T-shirts just proved that. She was prissy and neat and didn't want even a grain of sand on the floor. He was a free soul who didn't need a high school English teacher in his world. Even if they did form a relationship, within two years she'd be telling him they couldn't come to Florida anymore in the summer. When children came, there would be summer baseball, dancing classes, all those things that would put his free soul in a cage secured with a heavy pad lock.

He stole a glance toward the front of the store. The noise was deafening. Dixie kept moving and straightening shirts. She'd kicked off her sandals and worked in her bare feet. Her dark hair had come loose from the ponytail and fell in loose strands around her face. He wanted nothing more than to go up there and apologize for his rashness, brush the hair behind her ears with the tips of his fingers, take her chin in his palm and kiss her. For a moment he could feel the warmth of her lips on his, but it vanished and the heat of anger replaced it. Lord Almighty, what was he thinking? It was just the fact that they'd been working so closely all summer. That he'd built a silly castle with her and enjoyed a luau. Distance would take care of the problem. Out of sight, out of mind, so the old adage went. In a few more weeks, he'd go home to San Antonio and she'd go on back to her place in Arkansas. They'd never see each other again and in a few years, he'd even forget her name.

Dixie finished moving everything up to a higher level, then rummaged through her satchel and found the book she'd been reading. She scanned through the first hundred pages hurriedly to refamiliarize herself with the plot and had barely settled into the plastic lawn chair when a shotgun blast made her jump so high the chair fell backward, sending the book flying across the room and causing the electricity to go out. She was thrust into darkness so thick she couldn't see anything at all.

"You okay, Dixie?" Boone's worried voice came from the back of the store.

"I'm fine. Thought for a split second there Anita had come back with a shotgun," she said.

"Haven't seen her since you dragged the preacher man through here," he said. "That was just the electricity going. Probably a transformer and the whole block or more is without power. However, I can remedy that."

Dixie's eyes opened wider and wider, trying to focus on anything other than bizarre darkness in the middle of a summer afternoon. The muscles began to twitch, then she heard and saw a match at the same time. Boone lit two big round candles sporting three wicks each. She'd never seen light look so good.

"That ended my painting for the day. No electricity. No airbrush," he said.

"Maybe it will blow past in a few minutes and the electricity will come back on," she told him, picking her way gingerly from the front of the store to the back, the flames drawing her like a moth.

"What the?" She stopped after three steps and looked down. Water was seeping under the door and around the flap, streaming down the wall to the floor. Half an inch covered the floor and was rapidly making its way back to Boone's work post. "Boone, is every-thing up off the floor back there? We've got a flood."

"All up at least a foot. Never known it to get higher than that," he said. "Come on back here. We'll prop ourselves up here on the drying table and wait it out. It's all we can do anyway."

She followed his example and hopped backward up onto an old chrome kitchen table. She drew her feet up under her and watched mesmerized as the water deep-ened. "So has this happened before?"

"Sure, see the marks on the legs of the table?" He pointed down.

"Which ones?" she asked, leaning forward and hav-ing to catch herself before she toppled right off.

"All of them. The bottom four inches are the worst. See how the chrome is all gone and only the rusty metal remains. That's the storms I've weathered. Four or five of them. Never have lost electricity, though," he said.

"And the ones up higher?" she asked, a chill playing chase down her spine.

"Guess the water was about four feet high in here when that big series of hurricanes hit. Landlord said it was a wonder he didn't lose the old shack altogether. Must have petrified wood in here for it to hold up dur-ing that blow," Boone told her.

"So you rent the place?" Dixie watched the flicker-ing candle flames.

"Sublet. The owner goes to Colorado during the hot summer. He runs a shirt shop when I'm not here," Boone said.

"How could he make a living in the winter?" Dixie asked.

"Oh, darlin', he makes enough during spring break alone to live on all year with his lifestyle. He's a worse beach bum than I am," Boone said.

"Then why is he in Colorado during the hottest part of the season?" she asked.

"That's where his roots are. He was born and raised on a farm near Colorado Springs. Goes home for the summer every year and comes back telling me he's never going back, but come the next spring he's on the phone wanting to know if I'm ready to sublet," Boone said.

Dixie nodded. She understood. Every May she swore if she could find a job digging ditches or holding one of those SLOW signs for the highway department, she'd take it rather than go back to the classroom. But by the end of July she was always eager to get another school year started.

"How's the feud between Jill and Faith?" Boone asked.

"There's no feud. We're all best friends. We settled the whole affair that night before we went to bed," Dixie told him.

"I can't believe it," Boone chuckled. "I'd have sworn there would be a bloodletting after all us men folks went home. At the least, some hair pulling or shouting."

"No, that's not the way the club works," Dixie said.

"What club?" Boone's curiosity was piqued. He'd been right. They were a bunch of old maid school-teachers who belonged to some kind of women's organization. He'd bet his brand-new eel cowboy boots it was one of those new ones where they wore red hats and met once a week with some kind of secret password.

"It's nothing," Dixie said.

"You said a club. Tell me about it," he said.

"Okay, but remember you asked. Five years ago when we were all new teachers in Greenbrier, we got together one evening for a movie and sandwiches. We watched *Steel Magnolias*. Ever seen it?" she asked.

"Only about a dozen times. It's a chick-flick. My sisters-in-law love it. My mother loves it. Seems like every woman I've dated since it came out wants to rent it and watch it with me," he said.

"Something wrong with that?" She drew her eyes down and turned slightly to stare at the smug little look on his face. "I suppose you'd rather watch *Die Hard* a dozen times?"

"Of course," he muttered, unable to blink. He'd never seen her dark green eyes twinkle so brightly. Maybe it was the reflection of the candles. Suddenly, he leaned forward, tucked his fist under her chin and his mouth covered her mouth with his. The roar stopped and behind his closed eyes everything lit up like sugar sand glowing in a bright noonday sun.

Dixie wasn't prepared for the explosion of emotions rattling through her heart and soul. She wasn't a sophomore in high school. This wasn't her first kiss, but the way it made her heart skip around in her chest, it might as well have been. One thing for sure, Boone Callahan knew his way around the kissing business.

"I'm sorry," he pulled away and scooted aside, putting a foot of air between them.

"Why?" she asked. She wasn't a bit sorry.

"Because I shouldn't have done that. We have to work together and it will make things strange between us," he said. So much for forgetting Dixie. His lips were still on fire and begging for more.

"I see. Well, I'm not sorry, Boone, and if things are strange it will be because you make them that way. The kiss was nice but don't worry I'm not going to spend my time back here leaning over the table swooning at you. We're adults, not teenagers," she said.

"You got that right. It was the moment. Candles. The roar of a the storm. Now you were telling me about *Steel Magnolias*," he cleared his throat.

"We watched it that night and decided we'd be the steel magnolias of Greenbrier," she said. "Then when *The Divine Secrets of the Ya-Ya Sisterhood* came out we watched it and . . ."

"And I've seen that one, too. It's the most boring, stupid movie I've ever seen. So what if Sandra Bullock had a traumatic childhood. She should have gotten over it by the time she was thirty years old, wouldn't you think?" Boone said.

"Some things leave a deep impression and aren't so easy to get over," Dixie argued. How could he be so tender one minute and as obstinate as a longhorn steer the next?

"Seems to me both those women needed to wake up and face life. Good grief, that Viv character would give a psychiatrist hives. And her poor husband. He was as crazy as she was for staying with her. I'd have already filed for divorce years before," Boone said.

"Oh?" Dixie raised a dark eyebrow and glared at him. "Sounds like you're one of those suds-in-the-bucket men at heart after all, Boone."

"What's that supposed to mean? Are you comparing me to that sorry excuse you dated a whole year?" His temper flared higher than the candle flames.

"I am. When push comes to shove, you are all alike. Just divorce the woman if she's got problems with a horrible past and has trouble getting over it. And by all means, keep them in an apron bent over a washtub in the backyard," she smarted off to him.

"I don't think a woman has to do the laundry over a washtub. I believe in modern appliances," he raised his voice an octave.

"Don't you shout at me. It doesn't change the way you really feel. Siddalee had a right to be angry, to . . ."

". . . Are we arguing over a movie?" he asked.

"We're arguing over issues," she said. "It has nothing to do with the Ya-Ya's."

"What issues?" he asked.

"The issue of what you really feel in your heart about women," she said.

"I feel that a woman can work if she wants. She can make her own decisions. If she can do a man's job then she deserves a man's pay," he said.

"Well, how sweet of you, Boone Callahan," she all but snorted. "And if a man can do a woman's job, does he get the same pay? I'm going home."

"I'd like to see you try in that storm," he laughed at her.

The sound of his derisive guffaw was absolutely the straw that broke the old proverbial camel's back. She hopped down off the table into two inches of water, slopped her way to the front of the store and picked up her sandals from the countertop. She shoved them down into her satchel and marched to the front door.

"You are as crazy as that woman in that silly chick-flick if you walk out that door. If you're that crazy you don't need to be working for me," Boone yelled from his safe and dry perch on the chrome table.

"Darlin'," she shouted from the front door, "you can't fire this crazy woman. She just quit. Good-bye, Boone."

The force of the door flying open when she released the lock almost shot her to the back of the shop. Pure anger kept her glued to her spot in ankle-deep salt water. Grayness covered everything outside. Gray ocean water lapped all the way to the road. Gray skies. Gray rain. Gray mood in Dixie's heart. Using every bit of her might, she pulled the door shut behind her and began the fight against the wind as she made her way down the sidewalk toward home.

Tears of fear, bewilderment, and heartache mingled with the driving rain on her cheeks. She heard Boone screaming her name from the doorway and turned to see him motioning for her to come back. Well, he could stand there until the rain melted his salty old hide; she would never go back there. She trudged on toward home, soaked to the skin and getting hungrier by the minute.

Boone finally shut the door. He wasn't going to beg the woman. A little good wet rain might cool down that temper of hers. Drat her anyway for getting under his skin. And he never did get the rest of the story about their silly club where they all wore red hats and acted like little girls. He touched his lips. One kiss. He kicked the plastic chair with his bare foot and bloodied a toe.

One kiss.

And he wanted more just like it.

Chapter Eleven

W hat was usually no more than a leisurely fifteen-minute walk home took half an hour in the worst driving rain Dixie had ever been caught out in. Visibility was less than two feet. By the time she reached the front door of the beach house, she was exhausted. She threw open the door and then closed it just as fast, standing on the foyer tiles, dripping from the top of her head down to her bare feet.

"Good lord, Dixie, what are you doing home? Why didn't you stay at the T-shirt shop? Where is Boone? We don't have electricity," Faith said.

"Boone kissed me and I quit my job. I'm hungry," Dixie's face skewed up and she buried her face in her hands.

"You get the towels," Jill took charge, motioning to Faith.

"I'm all wet," Dixie threw back her head and regained her composure to some measure. It wasn't the fight with Boone, anyway. It was that long, harrowing walk home with the wind trying to blow her all the way to Oz. "It's raining so hard."

"Boone let you walk home all alone in that hurricane?" Jill took the satchel from her hands. "Bend over," she wrapped Dixie's hair in a towel. "Now strip out of those wet things. You'll catch pneumonia."

Dixie peeled out of her dripping clothes and wrapped herself in one of the towels Faith held out to her. "My terry robe is on the hook in my bathroom," she said.

Faith fetched it quickly. Dixie handed her the wet towels and put on her worn old robe, taking comfort in the dry warmth of it. "I think I've quit dripping. Thank you both."

"Get another spoon," Jill told Faith.

"Ice cream already out? What's going on?" Dixie noticed for the first time that both Jill and Faith had been crying.

"Come sit down," Faith pulled Dixie into the living room where two spoons stuck out of a brand-new container of ice cream. Sinful double chocolate. Well, it was sure an occasion for sinful chocolate.

Faith stuck another spoon in the ice cream. "Why did you quit your job if Boone kissed you? Did you find out he was married or what?"

"No, he kissed me and it was wonderful and I liked it and I wanted more," Dixie said then started to eat, one bite after another. "Is this all we've got? I'm really, really mad. Matter of fact, I think I'm madder right now than I was when Todd said I couldn't come to Florida with y'all."

"I've got a pot of gumbo on the stove. Just finished it when the electricity blew. When we finish this we'll eat every bite of it," Faith said.

"He was itching for a fight when I got to work. All snappy and slinging things around," Dixie said.

"Anita been back?" Jill asked.

"He says he hasn't seen her since I dragged the preacher in there, and those are his words, not mine. When I got there he looked blacker than the skies out over the ocean. He told me to go home before the storm hit, but I wanted to stay and help get the things up high in case of flooding. Then it was too late and everything went black. He lit a couple of candles and we were sitting on the drying table." She began to laugh, a nervous giggle that didn't sound humorous at all. "That's because the water was coming in on the floor. And he asked if you two were having a feud and I told him we didn't have feuds. It was against club rules."

"She's lost it," Faith said. "We'll have to get out the straightjacket and call for the room with the pink elephants on the walls if she doesn't stop that cackling like a witch."

"Or an old hen right after she's laid an egg," Jill said.

Dixie stopped as suddenly as she'd begun. "Hush, both of you. It's just funny looking back on it. Not ha-ha funny, but weird funny. It was as if he got all mad at himself, even more than he had been before the storm hit, just for kissing me. Talk about having a hard time figuring out women. Men are twice as bad. They're all intense and won't talk about what's really on their minds," she dipped into the ice cream, bringing up close to a double dip on the end of the spoon and set about eating it as if she was sentenced to the gallows and it was her last meal. Why had he gotten so angry over the movies, anyway? She couldn't begin to fathom why; probably a good psychiatrist would have trouble understanding it.

"Boone was just spoiling for a fight," Jill nodded seriously. "Anything would have set him off. My husband got like that sometimes. He'd get all edgy about something and the next thing we were fighting about meat loaf or whether to prune the roses that week or not. Once we even had it out over the way I placed the napkin on his plate for dinner."

"I didn't do anything. I liked his kiss, but then we started talking about the Ya-Ya's and he got all defensive saying both Siddalee and Viv were crazy and should grow up and face life. Then we were arguing," Dixie said.

"And he fired you over a silly argument about a movie?" Jill asked.

"No, he said if I walked out the door I was as crazy as those women in the movie and he didn't need a crazy woman working for him," Dixie said. "So I told him that this crazy woman was quitting and I walked out."

"It's the pull of this blasted hurricane. The sun is out of sync with the moon and Mars is all messed up this week anyway, which explains part of their stupidity. Doesn't excuse it but makes it understandable. Because they are from Mars their world is all upside down when

Mars is out of sync with the rest of the planets. Their hearts begin to love and is scares them so badly they go into battle mode," Faith wiped her eyes.

Dixie patted Faith on the shoulder. "Oh, darlin', don't cry. None of them are worth tears. Especially not Boone Callahan. That worthless man just showed his colors. I only thought I wanted to take his sorry hide home. He's shown me that he's no better than Todd. I should throw myself on the mercy of Morgan Chase and beg him for a second chance. I bet I could convince him to have a late-life baby with me and I could learn to be a really good grandmother to his grandchild."

"You a grandmother. Now that's a scary thought. A mother, yes, but none of us are ready for grandparenting. Besides, she's not crying for you," Jill wiped away a tear with the back of her hand, leaving a streak of chocolate on her cheek. "She's crying for herself, just like I am."

"What happened?" Dixie stopped licking the ice cream from the spoon.

"I told you it's the moon and this wicked storm. It's pulling their common sense out of their hearts and making them all loups-garous—that would be were-wolves. We need to make gris-gris bags to hide in their beds to bring them to their senses," Faith said.

"You two been fighting, too?" Dixie cocked her head to one side.

"Jackson is an old bear today. He was working on a game thing and I . . ." Faith's chin quivered.

"Jackson hurt your feelings?" Dixie asked.

"It's because I told him I was almost ten years older

than he is. I know that's what it really is. I was just asking if he had everything to make a shrimp scampi and whether I needed to run to town before the storm hit or if he'd rather I just made omelets for lunch. Then he got all huffy and said I needed to be quiet so he could concentrate," Faith said stoically. "That wasn't the real problem though. I told him yesterday about my real age and he said it didn't matter one bit to him, but it did. I should never have told him."

"He already knew so that's not the problem," Dixie said. "The first night I met him, he told me he'd seen your driver's license when you showed him a picture and had already figured it out. So he's really angry about something other than that."

"Then why didn't he tell me he knew? Why didn't you?" Faith asked.

"Because he asked me not to tell you. He said you'd tell him when you were ready and it didn't matter anyway, that he really liked you. So I didn't, but I guess I should have, huh?" Dixie patted her shoulder.

"Oh, it doesn't matter, now. But what else could it be? It's another woman, isn't it?" Faith grabbed a tissue.

"Who knows?" Dixie hugged Faith.

"Jill, too," Faith sobbed. "That low-down swamp rat Travis Paul Beauchamp hurt her feelings."

"Well, get me some black candles," Dixie declared. "I don't know one blessed thing about voodoo but I betcha I can fashion up some little dolls and find some straight pins. I know exactly where I'm going to stick my little Boone doll."

"Paul wanted me to fly to Los Angeles with him

Monday and be gone until Friday. I told him I couldn't because we have a meeting every Monday night and we'd already missed several and I wouldn't miss another one and I'd fly out on Tuesday and . . ." She put up her hands in dismissal, picked up the spoon and dug all the way to the bottom of the ice cream.

"But our Monday could've been tomorrow night," Dixie said.

"No, it couldn't. He had no right to demand that I jump through hoops and give up what's important to me. He was spoiling for a fight just like Jackson and Boone. They're just being one hundred percent bonafide jackasses. I don't know anything about all that astrology or where the planets are lined up. I think Paul is testing the waters to see if I'll bend to his every will," Jill said. "He told me I was putting my friends before our relationship and he said that we were acting like teenagers with our little girlfriend club. He was just plain mean."

Dixie scraped the bottom corners of the ice cream cartoon and licked her spoon clean. "Boone said something like that and he didn't even know the whole story of the PMS Club. I didn't get that far. When I mentioned the Ya-Ya's, he went off into a temper fit. I'm ready for gumbo now. Got any of that garlic bread to go with it."

"She's really upset." Faith had mascara running down her cheeks and her own thick blond hair was hanging in limp locks.

"Did you come home in the rain, too?" Dixie asked.

"Oh, yes, but I only had to run across the beach a little ways. Of course I could have been swept into the ocean and drowned and Jackson wouldn't have cared. After all, I'm just an old woman he's used up and is ready to throw away like so much garbage," Faith intoned dramatically. "I will burn black candles and wicked incense for him. And I'll help you make those little dolls, Dixie. Jill, you're the one who packed everything but the bathroom sink for this trip. You did bring a sewing needle and some straight pins, didn't you?"

"Of course. Can you believe that Paul got all riled over my friendship with you two?" Jill dipped up a bowl of gumbo, looked at it a minute, then added another cupful. Forget about watching her weight. If she weighed fifty more pounds when she went back to Greenbrier she'd just go shopping.

"Yes, I can," Faith said. "He's going to steal your identity."

"Oh, he is not. He's just mad at something else and is taking it out on you," Dixie came to his rescue as she pulled another hunk of bread loose and began to eat in earnest. "He's worried about what Faith might tell you."

"Well, he should be," Faith helped herself to the gumbo and bread, carrying it to the living room. She folded her long legs up under her and sat on the floor in front of the coffee table. "How can we eat when our hearts have been broken?"

"Easy. Put one bite in and chew," Dixie said sarcastically.

"I'm putting my periapt back on and I'm wearing it the whole rest of the summer," Faith said. "I do declare, mumbo jumbo, hickory dickory dock, and all the other chants I never could remember, that from this moment on, they will protect us from mischief and illness."

"You already had chicken pox," Dixie almost smiled.

"Well, I'm not getting mumps and I'm sure not ever going to speak to good looking men on the beach again. I'm going home to Greenbrier and finding a man who appreciates a mature rich woman, one who licks her toes every day just to show how much he needs her," Faith said.

"That sounds a bit kinky to me," Dixie said.

"Oh, be quiet, it's figurative. Not literal," Faith hissed. "If food was like alcohol, I'd be ready to pass out about now. I'm going to my room to curl up under the blankets. I may sleep until morning. If Jackson were to happen to call, tell him I said for him to drop dead and rot."

"Me, too," Jill put her empty bowl in the sink. "If it don't stop in a while and you need some help building an ark, wake me up, Dixie. But other than that, I don't care if Paul arrives stark naked with a bouquet of red roses and is singing my favorite song, don't wake me up. Tell him to run along to California and find a beach bunny with only one brain cell to keep him company."

"What's your favorite song?" Dixie asked with a wicked grin on her face.

"Why?" Jill stopped in her doorway.

"Because I just want to know what he'll be singing. And am I allowed to listen until he finishes or do I just kick him off the porch and into the rain when he starts singing? And can I keep the roses or do I throw them at his naked butt when he's leaving?"

Jill began to giggle and Faith joined in. Before long they were all three holding their sides and roaring.

"Guess we are a bunch of high school sophomores in a silly girlfriend club," Jill said. "But Paul Beauchamp will go to his grave never knowing I said that."

"So will Jackson Smith," Faith said.

"Not Boone. I'll tell him to his face and watch him explode. I'll even tell him he just kissed jailbait," Dixie stopped laughing and her mood turned dark again. "I think I'll have another bowl of gumbo. Not to worry, my PMS friends. I will keep careful watch over our dark and dreary castle. No knights in shining armor or even stable boys will make it through the front door this day."

"Thank you," Jill and Faith said in unison.

Dixie loosened the ties of her robe and propped her feet up on the coffee table. They had acted more than a little bit like teenagers, but it was just the youthful, feminine side of their nature. The one men would never understand. Speaking of which, Boone hadn't acted so mature himself. Had the kiss scared him out of his wits? Goodness only knew if Anita was the run of the mill for what he usually kissed, he wouldn't want to be kissing someone like Dixie. Short, dark-haired, green-eyed, eyebrows that were too heavy, a sassy attitude and blunt speech. It was a wonder he didn't try to wipe the kiss off his lips. Come to think of it, he did reach up and touch his mouth when he pulled back.

She'd put Boone and the whole ugly argument from her mind and read a few chapters of her book by candlelight. Her book! She moaned when she remembered tossing it up in the air when the electricity went off. No doubt it had fallen on the floor and was a soggy mess by now. She'd never know if the woman in the tower married that wicked duke and submitted to him to produce an heir. Or if she finally found the courage to run away with the Irishman.

Todd was the duke. He'd had the love of his life in his first marriage. Had done up the whole thing in extravagant style. The southern belle of all Arkansas. The big wedding at the family estate in Little Rock. Then she'd died and now all he wanted was a woman willing to do his bidding and produce a little Todd Riley 5th, or was it 6th?

Dixie was the maiden in the tower; the guards, her fears. Fears keeping her in the cold, high room. She'd think about that idea tomorrow. Tonight she just wanted to figure out how a woman truly knew which man was the right one?

Boone could be the Irishman but in the book the Irishman loved the maiden in the tower. Lord save a maiden in distress if Boone really ever did fall in love with her. If a kiss could set him off like that, imagine how bullheaded he'd get if he ever fell for a woman. No, Boone wasn't the Irishman. He was a warrior. Maybe if her book wasn't totally ruined she'd find a twist in the plot. The true hero wasn't the Irishman at all, but the warrior. The warrior whose ancestors came from Mars and the only woman who could tame him was the blond . . . *well, damn it anyway,* she thought. That heroine was blond! Maybe Dixie should find Anita and let her in on the secret that Boone wasn't married and turn that witch back loose on him. She might very well be the only woman who could tame that wicked temper of his.

And who can tame yours? that niggling little voice she hated said loudly.

"It'll take someone very special to tame my temper or else I'd better marry a chef," she whispered as she got up off the sofa, stretched and went to watch the downpour from the patio doors leading out the back. There'd been little let-up since she'd got home. Everything still looked and felt gray. The ocean water had a foaming on top on it and Sara Evans' song about suds in the bucket came to mind again.

She wondered what Boone was doing perched on his chrome table with two candles. Nothing to read. No radio to listen to his country music. No friends to talk about why he was so angry or to tell what a crazy thing Dixie had done when she plowed right out into that storm. Not one thing but his thoughts to keep him company. Dixie leaned against the glass. The coolness felt good but did little to ease the emptiness in her heart.

A tear brimmed up on her lower lashes and hung for a long time before it traveled slowly down her cheek. She'd actually quit her job. The next four weeks loomed out there like a big, black cloud. Faith and Jackson would make up. In a couple of days they'd be keeping the grass in the pathway between the two houses worn away. There was a very good possibility Paul and Jill would straighten out their argument. But she and Boone didn't have a foundation to build on once the fighting words settled.

She wiped away the tear while it dangled on her chin. No more. She hadn't cried for Todd and she'd wasted a whole year on him. Why should she cry for Boone when all they'd shared was one electrifying kiss?

Chapter Twelve

The phone ringing snapped Dixie out of a deep sleep where she'd curled up on the sofa. Her neck ached from the odd angle she'd propped it on the sofa's arm. She rubbed it and tried to ignore the insistent noise. Maybe Faith or Jill would answer it. After ten rings she reached above her head and picked up the remote phone.

"Hello," she said grumpily. Nothing but more ringing. She held the phone out and looked at it quizzically. Then she remembered that the electricity was out and the cordless didn't work without it. She stomped down the hallway and grabbed the wall phone. "Hello," she almost shouted.

"Dixie, is that you?" Todd's voice came through loud and clear.

158

"Yes, what are you doing calling here in the middle of the night?" she asked bluntly.

"It's not the middle of the night. Are you drunk? It's only eight o'clock. I heard there was a bad storm down there and I was just calling to check on you," Todd said.

"No, I'm not drunk, unless you can get drunk on rain water and ice cream. And we are fine so don't worry about us," she said.

"Have you come to your senses yet? Ready to make up and get married?" he asked.

"I thought I'd dry up an old maid if I walked out the door," she told him.

"Oh, honey, we were fighting. People say things they don't mean when they're arguing. But then when they've had some time adults cool down and realize it was just a fight, nothing to end a whole relationship over," he said with a soft laugh.

Dixie held the phone out from her ear and stared at it. "Are you apologizing? Have you had a change of heart about me working?" she asked when she put it back to her ear.

"No, I'm not apologizing. It wasn't my idea for you to run off all summer and you won't ever do such a silly thing again. You're not a college sorority girl off to the beach on spring break. For crying out loud, you are a grown woman. And I've certainly not had a change of heart about you working. You'll stay home and be ready to do what we need to do as a philanthropic family. It takes a lot of time to be civic- and community-minded. I just thought I'd given you enough time to rethink your decision and come on home. We could run over to the courthouse, get married and still have time for a decent honeymoon. How about Hawaii?" Todd said.

"There's not that much time left in the world. Good-bye, Todd," she said and put the receiver back on the hook.

She padded softly back to the window. The rain had let up considerably. Now it was a steady downpour but the wind had died down. She could see the ocean better. It was still soapy looking as it made its way forward and backward. The nerve of Todd Riley to act more like her father than the man she thought she wanted to marry. Had he really called or was it part of a crazy, mixed up dream. No, she'd talked to him, all right, and he was of the opinion that if he waited long enough, she'd come home all ready to make up with him. Evidently Mars was out of sync in Arkansas as well as Florida. She put her nose to the glass, squinting in hopes that she could see a break in the clouds, and left a foggy circle where she exhaled. She blinked and then squealed. In the blurred vision, she thought she saw a man's nose on the other side of the glass. She took two steps backward, blinked a couple of times, and sure enough the man was still there.

"Jackson," she mumbled as she opened the sliding doors.

"Hello, Dixie," Boone said from the deck. "I rang the doorbell out front a dozen times but no one answered. Got worried so I . . ."

His blond hair hung in his face and there couldn't be

one dry thread on him. His brown eyes did indeed look worried.

"We're all fine. The doorbell won't work because the electricity is out. Remember?" she said.

"Then I'll leave. I . . ."

"Oh, come on in but stop right there on the tile while I get some towels," she said. Might as well get all the men problems finished in one evening. First Todd. However, he had said something that made sense. In adult relationships arguments didn't mean the end of the whole affair. It just meant sitting on the time-out chair awhile until tempers cooled and the adults were rational again. Dixie knew that. She'd been in relationships before and there had been arguments. But this was different. Todd Riley thought he was God.

She threw two towels across the room at Boone and sat down on the sofa to watch as he attempted to get dry. In that wet T-shirt and those cut-off jeans, he could dance on the stage of a strip joint for the ladies and make a mint. "Is this going to take long?" she asked.

"Maybe," he answered.

"Then I'd suggest you go down the hall to the second door on the right to the bathroom. Uncle Vincent or some feller who's been here left a big terry robe on a hook right inside the door. You might want to shed all those wet clothes and borrow that robe. Just throw them over the towel rack. You think they'll be dry by the time you're ready for them again?" she asked.

"Depends. If it's still raining it won't matter, but I

would appreciate a dry robe for a little while," he said seriously and walked toward the bathroom.

She waited.

Before he went back to face Dixie, he took time to comb his hair back with his fingertips and look in the mirror. The miserable man looking back at him needed to shave. Didn't seem fair. Blond hair and a heavy beard. An oxymoron. Blond haired men usually didn't have a chest full of hair or need to shave twice a day either.

"I wanted to apologize," he said simply when he lowered himself into an overstuffed leather chair.

"I told you at the time. I enjoyed that kiss so no apology is necessary," she said.

"Not about that. I should apologize for that, too. I should have never said I was sorry I kissed you. That was the biggest lie I've told in years. I wasn't sorry. I wanted to kiss you for a long time. I came to tell you I'm sorry for letting you go out in that storm alone. You could have been killed if there had been an exposed electrical wire anywhere, or blown all the way to China, as small as you are and the way the wind was whipping those trees around. And besides, the whole fight wasn't your fault, it was mine," he said.

"Oh?" she raised an eyebrow. A man who took the blame for his own actions. Now that was a nice change from the usual. Most of them would have turned the whole thing around to be her fault because she was as crazy as Viv and Siddalee in the movie.

"You're not going to make this easy are you?" He looked directly into her green eyes.

"No, I'm not. I was trying to tell you about our club and you went off like a bottle rocket," she said. "So keep talking."

"Please don't quit working for me," he said. "I like working with you and I like you, Dixie. We work well together and this has been the best summer I've ever had."

"Business or pleasure?" she asked.

"Both," he didn't blink and neither did she, their eyes locked together, sparks flying in the distance between them.

"I owe you an explanation," he finally looked out the window at the steady rain. "Every year my family comes down here the first week of August. The whole family. All the brothers, their wives and kids, and my mom and dad. It's the highlight of my whole summer. They're in and out of the shop. Sometimes the women run the shop for an afternoon and let us guys play on the beach with the kids. I got a phone call this morning before you came to work. There's been a change of plans. Crock and his family have decided to go to Disneyland in California this year rather than come to Florida. The kids want something different. Sam's kids have gotten involved in summer league ball and their schedule won't work. Mom and Dad have decided to take a couple of weeks and go to the East Coast all alone. And Bowie's family decided to go to Colorado to the mountains this year. I was already angry when you got to work. Just looking for something to vent on and you were there," he said.

"Thank you," she said.

"For venting on you and saying all those mean things," he said.

"No, for being honest, Boone. Thank you for that. And I will be at work at three tomorrow afternoon, but I think most of what we'll be doing is bailing water," she tried to smile but it was weak.

Boone would take weak if that's the best he could get. He'd spent hours perched up on his chrome throne, mulling over the whole day like a Texas hound dog with a ham bone. When the anger had spent itself, he realized he'd been a fool. To take out his frustrations on Dixie had been uncalled for at best. He should have told her exactly why he was irritable when she first arrived, then the whole argument could have been avoided.

"I'll go retrieve my wet things then and go home," he said.

"You don't have to," she said.

He cocked his head off to one side and looked at her. What was she offering?

"The sofa is short but it sure beats walking home in the rain. Faith and Jill are so emotionally drained that they'll sleep until morning. So will I. So the sofa is yours if you want to use it. I was on my way to bed when you scared the bejesus out of me," she nodded toward the window.

"Thank you, but did you tell the girls at your club thing about our fight?" he asked sheepishly.

"Yes, I did. There's very little I keep from Jill and Faith. We had an unofficial meeting of the Periapt Magnolia Sisterhood when I got home. I ate the better part of a half gallon of sinfully double chocolate ice cream, two bowls of gumbo and a half a loaf of garlic bread before my mad spell became tameable," she said.

"They'll slit my throat in my sleep," he said.

"Maybe, so you'd better get up before they do," she said sassily as she went to her bedroom. "Don't sleep too soundly, Boone."

"Good night to you, too, Dixie," he smiled, his eyes twinkling.

"Good night," she whispered and shut the door behind her, sliding down the back side. Comparing people wasn't right. But how could she not, when she'd only barely told Todd there wasn't enough time in the world and then there was Boone on the other side of the glass? Todd with his condescending, higher-and-mightier-than-thou attitude. Nothing had changed. Come on home and we'll still do it my way. Boone with his sincere apology. She looked through the windows of her soul and there was Boone, center stage in a borrowed robe, soft blond fur peeking out where it gaped open over his chest. He'd said he liked her. That was a first step. Maybe she would take him home after all.

Rain pounded on Dixie's window when she awoke but the alarm clock flashed twelve o'clock over and over again. The aroma of coffee and bacon mixed together filled the room. Evidently the electricity had been repaired even if the rain hadn't stopped. She threw off the sheet and her robe, found a pair of underpants, some faded denim shorts, a bra and a tank top. She didn't bother to brush her hair or even look in the mirror. She just followed her nose to the kitchen where she figured Faith was making breakfast.

"Good morning, sleepy head," Faith said from a table laden with breakfast food. "How could you sleep so long with all these wonderful smells?"

"Dixie?" Boone said from the kitchen. "Did you sleep well?"

"Boone!" She sat down at the table to keep from falling. She expected him to be gone by the time she, Jill and Faith arose that morning. She sure didn't expect to see him right at home in the kitchen making breakfast. Or for him to see her without her hair even combed. At that thought, her hand went to her hair to find a rat's nest at the nape of her neck.

"You look lovely this morning. Help yourselves. Don't wait for me. I'm still working on the rest of this pancake batter and then I'll eat. But please know that I get all the leftovers so you'd better eat your fill before you leave the table," he grinned.

"Why did you do this?" Dixie asked.

"Don't look a gift horse in the mouth," Jill shook a fork at her. "We haven't had breakfast like this in forever. Look, he's even made grits."

"Do you give lessons? I'll sign Jackson up if you do," Faith said.

The traitors, Dixie thought. Feed them some crispy bacon, grits, hash browns and hot biscuits with sausage gravy and they turned their backs on her. Sold out for a pottage called breakfast.

"Are you still mad?" Faith frowned. "Because if you are, I want two more biscuits before you get started."

"No, I'm over that mad and working up a new one," Dixie whispered.

"At us? He told us he apologized and you let him sleep on the sofa and borrow Uncle Vincent's robe until his clothes dried. He had breakfast started when we came out of our rooms and we thought he was telling the truth," Jill whispered right back.

Dixie smiled brightly. "He was. Don't hoard the biscuits, Faith. Let's see if he can make them as good as my momma can."

"Oh, sugar, you are in for a surprise. These would make your momma's look like hard tack on a cattle drive."

"Flattery will get you anything you want," Boone said from the kitchen. "This is a real treat, getting to cook in a full-sized kitchen for more than one person."

"You mean you'd do this often if you had a big kitchen?" Dixie asked.

"I do. Cook on Sunday morning before church for my whole family. That's my tradition. Sunday dinner is at my folks' place," he said.

"Why hasn't some woman snatched you up before now?" Faith slathered butter over a stack of pancakes and covered them with maple syrup.

"Haven't found one yet that's willing for the Sunday morning tradition. When I do I'll let her snatch me right up," Boone put another platter of hot pancakes in the middle of the table, refilled coffee cups and then joined the women.

"Why wouldn't they be willing for a family tradi-tion?" Jill transferred two pancakes from the stack onto her plate. Be danged to the calories and fat grams. An opportunity like this didn't come by very often.

"Most women feel threatened by a man's family. They go into the relationship all sweet like honey pie and then get crazy. Suddenly the Sunday morning tradition interferes with their lifestyle. Sunday dinner at the folks' house is too big of a bite out of their schedule," he said.

"Anita?" Faith asked.

"That's right. Prime example. Guess you Periwack Magnolia Sisters do tell everything," he almost blushed.

"Periapt, as in a Tibetan amulet worn around the neck to prevent mischief and illness," Faith said. "Not Periwack."

"Apologies," Boone smiled but he was looking right at Dixie, not at Faith.

"Accepted. And we do tell one another a lot of things. It's our vent," Dixie told him.

"I see," Boone kept grinning as he helped his plate.

"So are you going to open the shop today?" Jill changed the subject. It had to be awkward for Boone and Dixie, knowing that everyone around the table was aware of the way Boone had acted.

"Oh, yes, it'll be open. Mostly though I expect Dixie and I'll spend most of the time cleaning up the flood mess," he said.

"But I thought you quit," Faith wished she could have taken the words the minute they were out of her mouth.

"I did, but my boss offered me my job back," Dixie couldn't keep the insane smile off her face. She must look like the tabby cat who'd finally found a way to get the gold fish out of the bowl.

"Well, you certainly can't go on foot in this rain. Take my car and there're umbrellas beside the door," Jill told them.

"Thanks, Jill," Dixie said. "But first I intend to eat."

The doorbell rang loud and clear several times before anyone could make a wise crack about hoping Dixie wasn't angry. "I'll get it," she wiped her mouth with a napkin and took off to the front of the house. "Shall I send him packing? You know it'll be either Jackson or Paul."

"Or Todd?" Faith was absolutely going to cut her tongue out by the roots.

"No, he called last night. Same offer. I refused," Dixie said over her shoulder as she opened the door.

Paul stood there, an umbrella in one hand, a bouquet of no less than two dozen red roses in the other. "Could I please speak to Jill?" His tone was humble and his face downright pitiful.

Dixie gritted her teeth to keep from giggling. "Perhaps. But give me that umbrella first."

"I will not. I'd be soaked in less than a minute," he declared.

"How bad do you want to talk to Jill?" She started to shut the door in his face.

Using the umbrella he blocked the doorway. "I want to talk to Jill very badly. I'd do about anything to make things right with her."

"Is that right?" Dixie grinned.

"Yes, it is," Paul said.

"Then I'll hold the roses and you'll take off that overcoat, suit coat, shirt, and are you wearing an under-shirt?" Dixie asked.

"Yes, I am but what business is that of yours, Dixie?" he asked.

"Take it off, too, and your shoes. I'm going to let you keep your pants though, for modesty's sake," she said.

"What is this all about?" Paul began to take off his clothes and wondered what in the devil he was letting the woman talk him into doing.

"You'll see," Dixie said.

"Who is it?" Faith called from the table. "Is it Jackson? Tell him to go drown himself in the ocean."

"Don't either of you leave the table," Dixie yelled back.

"Is she really still upset?" Paul stood in the pouring rain in nothing but his soaking wet trousers. Rain plastered his hair to his head and ran in rivulets down his cheeks.

"I would be if you'd said those things to me. Do you know the words to "The Rose"? That would be Jill's all time favorite song in the whole world. Can you do it like Conway Twitty?" Dixie asked.

"Better," Paul told her.

She handed him the roses and told him not to move, to stand in the rain, hold the roses, and when Jill opened the door to begin singing "The Rose," without taking his eyes off her. If she didn't slam the door in his face then he might have a chance to redeem himself.

"This is crazy," he said.

"So are those who belong to the Periapt Magnolia Sisterhood. Think you can live with that?" Dixie asked bluntly.

"I can live with anything but losing Jill. I've fallen in love with her," Paul said.

"Then give me to the count of twenty and ring the doorbell again," Dixie told him.

Paul nodded.

"Was it Jackson?" Faith asked when Dixie had taken her place back at the table.

"No, it was a man from the electric company making sure we had power. Right feisty little fellow. Asked me for a date," Dixie looked at Boone and winked.

"You stayed gone long enough to have gone on one with him," Jill snapped. Paul wasn't coming back. He wasn't even going to call. Was her place in the PMS Club truly worth losing the love of her life?

The doorbell rang again.

"Jackson!" Faith started to jump up only to feel Dixie kick her under the table.

"Why'd . . ." Faith looked across the table at Dixie who was smiling and winking.

"You get it Jill. Tell him this old woman can't find her walker and can't get to the door," Faith said. "And you, tell me what's going on?" she whispered to Dixie as soon as Jill was out of the kitchen.

A rich baritone voice with a sexy southern accent filtered down the hallway, singing "The Rose." Paul had been right, that Louisiana flavor did indeed give it even more life than Conway's version.

"Travis?" Faith shook her head.

"Paul. Jill's Paul. He's standing out there barefoot in nothing but his expensive slacks with two dozen roses in his arms, singing her favorite song. Think that will melt the ice around her heart?" Dixie asked.

"Travis?" Faith still couldn't believe it.

"No, Paul. Your Travis wouldn't have done that. But Jill's Paul would," Dixie told her. "Listen, the singing has stopped and the door is shut. Is that a sigh and a kiss I hear?"

"The world is coming to an end. It's going to flood again and wipe out all of mankind except us six, and one of them is Travis Paul Travis. Call the lumberyard and get us the boards to build an ark. This isn't happening." Faith grabbed a biscuit and disappeared into her room.

"Where's Paul?" Dixie asked when Jill came back to the table, the whole front of her shirt and shorts wet.

"He's in the bathroom, taking off his wet clothes and borrowing Uncle Vincent's robe." Jill's cheeks were as scarlet as the shirt she wore. "You told him to do that, didn't you?"

"Some things are never told even to the Sisterhood," Dixie said. "Give me the keys to the car and we'll get on out of here and give you some makeup time. Faith is in her room and Jackson will probably be here before long anyway. The electricity is back on so you can at least toss Paul's slacks and wet things in the dryer."

"Thank you. How could I really stay mad when Paul was standing there sopping wet, with roses, and singing my favorite song? Keys are on the hook. I'll call you at the shop later," she said.

"Well, he wasn't naked," Dixie said.

"Hush," Jill blushed again.

On the way out the door, Dixie literally ran into Jackson, bent against the rain and running without an umbrella, as soaked as Paul had been when Jill answered the door.

"Got something to say to Faith?" she asked when he was inside the house and dripping in the foyer. "She thinks this is about the age thing."

"It's not. I was upset over a game I've been working on for months. On the very day I finished it, my biggest competitor sold one exactly like it. I decided to change mine up enough to make it different and it was giving me fits," he said. "Where is she? I need to talk to her."

"In there, but I'd tread gently. She says to tell you to drop dead and rot in hell—or was the latest one to jump into the ocean and drown? Can't remember, there were lots of them," Dixie said.

"Thanks for the advice," Jackson said seriously, tip-toeing to Faith's room.

"Now why did you do that?" Boone asked when they were inside the car and the umbrellas stashed behind the seat. "You gave Paul a lot better fighting chance than that."

"He's young. He can wiggle his way out of it. Besides, Faith isn't as mad as Jill was. Not really. She's in there right now getting ready to go over to his house and apologize for being so short with him, too." Dixie put the key in the ignition and started the engine.

"How do you know that?" Boone asked.

"Periwack intuition," Dixie told him. "Do you think the storm will last all day?"

"Which one? The natural one or the other one?" He reached across the console and took her hand in his.

"Either one." She drove with her left hand and enjoyed the way his thumb made little circles on the soft web between her thumb and forefinger. He could easily hypnotize her in thirty minutes if he kept that up.

"Who knows what the future holds," he whispered.

Chapter Thirteen

Boone and Dixie looked around the shop. Things were back to normal and it was only mid-afternoon. They were totally exhausted, hungry and dirty but the place was clean. Gallons and gallons of sand swept from the floor before they hosed it down. T-shirts folded neatly and in the right bins. Everything put to order. They'd worked well together, discussing the job at hand rather than the bigger one in their hearts and minds.

The sun pushed around a few clouds and finally overcame the dreariness by shining brightly, the rain finally giving up completely and moving on north. Boone raised the window flap and set the cash register back in its rightful place. Bright sun filtered into the shop, along with hot muggy air. Boone's blond hair was already plastered to his forehead; Dixie's ponytail hung in limp strands, a few escaping to stick to her neck. Dirt smudges stained Boone's face; Dixie's didn't look a bit better. It felt like the humidity was five hundred percent and yet the sun was shining.

Dixie plopped down in her white plastic chair and wished for a long, cool shower. Or even a ten-minute dip in the still soapy looking ocean. But either would be a futile attempt to evade the humidity. Within two minutes after the shower or the dip, she'd be all sweaty again. Her stomach growled and she scanned the shelf right under the cash register where she usually kept a box of crackers. She found nothing but a book.

"My book!" Dixie exclaimed. "I thought I'd thrown it on the floor when the lights went out. I figured it was ruined from the flood."

"No, I found it right there after you left. Waded up here to see if there were any crackers in that box you keep under there. It was empty so I threw it away. Read the book and put it back," Boone said.

"You read this by the candlelight?" Dixie asked skeptically.

"Hey, I would have read Webster's dictionary, it got so boring in here. I just moved the candles to the drying table back there, stretched out on my stomach and read for hours. But you'd already told me about the first hundred pages so I just scanned through that part," he told her.

"What happened?" she asked.

"With the Irishman and Miss Bronwyn? Don't you want to read it for yourself? It's the only one you've got here and it's going to be a long, boring, hot day, Dixie. Everyone who was here for the weekend has already gone home. Those who were vacationing probably gave up when the storm hit and went home. Mondays are always slow but sales will be nil today," he said.

"Tell me what happens. I may still read it but I want you to tell me," she looked at the man on the cover of the book. He didn't look like Pastor Vance so much now that she really thought about it. Vance was pretty all right, but not in the sultry, raw way the hero was with all those muscles and steamy looking eyes.

"There's a twist in the middle of the book. Bronwyn thinks she's in love with the Irishman and he lets her think that until he rescues her. He's got a red-haired lass waiting for him in Ireland and he's there to convince her not to marry the duke. He does it by pretending to love her," Boone said.

"That rat. I knew I shouldn't trust an Irishman," she pursed her lips angrily.

"I'm Irish. You don't get much more Irish than Callahan," Boone told her.

"And your point is?" she asked mischievously. The mumbo jumbo, hickory dickory dock hadn't worked for her periapt, evidently.

"You can trust me, Dixie," he said so close to her that his warm breath caused goosebumps to rise up on her neck.

"Okay, okay, point taken. Then what happens?" she asked.

"The Irishman goes in as a priest so she could have confessional before her wedding. He gives her his robes and she walks right out past those guards disguised as a priest. Then he uses the rope he brought under the robes and repels out the window and down the side of the castle. He takes her to a ship and puts her on it. She and the ship's captain, a former warrior in the King's army, clash from day one, but before long she starts looking at him in a different light. By the time the ship reaches port, they are in love. The end."

"Why didn't the Irishman want her to marry the duke?" she asked.

"I told you the romantic part. You have to read it to get the lesson in history." He took her by the arm and turned her quickly, his mouth settling on hers in a deep kiss that shook his heart so hard it began to race.

"I'm not sorry for that one, either," she said breathlessly when he stepped back.

"Me, neither," he said.

"Hello, didn't know if any of the businesses would be open," a tall blond stepped through the door. "I'm glad to see you're open. I need to buy some shirts to take home to my nieces."

Boone started at her toes and went all the way to the top of her head. Now, that was the kind of woman he'd always envisioned himself waiting at the front of the church for. Long, thick blond hair. A figure that could wear any kind of wedding dress. Who'd be able to stand flatfooted and kiss him without having to balance on her tiptoes.

"Dixie, darlin', would you show her the book? I've probably got time to work up whatever she wants," Boone said.

"I'm sure you do," Dixie said icily.

"No, no," the lady said. "I don't have time to wait for

custom made. My husband and I are on our way home. Our honeymoon, you see. My five nieces were junior bridesmaids in the wedding. I want to bring them a surprise. Something off the racks will be fine."

Dixie pointed toward the walls. "Take your pick, then. They're all for sale."

"Oh, that's wonderful. Size doesn't matter. They're all small and would love one to use for a bathing suit cover-up." She quickly chose seven, deciding on two for herself.

"Now what did I do wrong?" Boone asked Dixie when the blond had paid out and was in the car waiting at the curb.

"Boone, I like you a lot. I really do. But I'm not your type. You all but salivated just looking at that woman. She could have been shaken out of the same mold Anita was poured into. I don't know where we're going with this but I do know that you never have looked at anyone short, dark-haired and green-eyed like you did that lady," Dixie said honestly. Women weren't supposed to discuss relationships when a friendship and two kisses was still in the fragile state. But she wasn't going to waste a whole year on anyone again only to find at the end they were as compatible as coyotes and chickens.

"You are right," he said.

Her heart dropped.

"I'll probably always admire pretty, tall women, but when I kiss you, Dixie, it's like you're the only woman in this world. And that's not a pickup line. I don't know where this is going, either. And I sure don't want to rush it. I don't want you to ever think you're a rebound woman since you're the first person I've felt anything for since Anita and I broke up," he said.

"I see." She picked up her book and hid behind it, trying to sort out whether she could live with that and Boone's roving eye.

"I'm going to paint a few shirts. If you want to talk, just let me know," he said.

She nodded. She read sixty pages before she looked up. Boone was both the Irishman and the warrior in the book. He was the Irishman, giving her a way out past her fears and demons just outside the door. Giving her honest answers to her questions. Rescuing her from a marriage of convenience like Todd offered. Then he was the ship's captain. All muscles, angry at times, taking her back to her rightful inheritance. Giving her space and time to make up her own mind. But sending her senses spinning with desire every time he was in the same room with her.

"I'm ready to talk," she laid the book aside and went back to the chrome table where two shirts were drying. She propped a hip on the edge of the table.

"And?" Boone kept painting.

"But first, I'm hungry. But for real. Not because I'm mad," she said. "I'm going down the street to see if the hot dog vendor is out today. You want onions and chili? My treat since you fixed breakfast."

"Hey, Jill got a song and flowers. No telling what Jackson ended up giving Faith. Breakfast was a small offering," he said.

"It was bigger than you think," she tiptoed and brushed a gentle kiss across his lips.

"Yes, chili and onions then and a root beer. The fridge is empty. I ate everything in it, which was two stale pieces of bread and a chunk of cheese and then drank all the sodas while I read that book yesterday," he said.

"It's yours," she grabbed her purse and left.

No sooner had she disappeared than Anita walked through the door. "So the little wifey has gone for the day? Come on Boone. I know you aren't married, so fess up."

"No, we aren't married. I lied to you to get you to leave me alone, Anita," he looked at all that blond, gorgeous beauty and suddenly it was as if the pretty outside melted away, showing the true woman inside, and the sight wasn't pretty at all.

"But Boone, darlin', we were made for each other. Can't you just see the wedding of the century? All of Texas would be agog for years," she crooned, leaning across the bar separating him from the rest of the store, showing him six inches of cleavage and a smile that would dazzle a monk.

"And you're going to move into my house in San Antonio? My little three-bedroom brick home on the outskirts of town with only twenty acres around it? You're going to be a ju-co professor's wife? You're going to have children and go to PTA meetings? Change diapers? Get up at three o'clock for feedings? Come here and live with me in an RV every summer?" He crossed his arms over his chest and waited.

"Of course not. I'd be a fool to say I'd do those things when I have no intention of ever doing them.

We'll be Mr. and Mrs. Beautiful Texans, Boone. You'll love what I'm offering if you'd just stop being so bull-headed and really think about it. Most men would jump at the chance for a lifetime of easy living as well as loving." She smiled her brightest.

"Anita, I don't love you. I thought I did. I thought you were the one for me, but I was wrong. I don't want to marry you," he said honestly.

"Well, darlin', I gave you one more chance. There's another one waiting in the wings anyway. He's not nearly as pretty but his bank account makes up for that. He won't look as good on the front of the magazines when they run the wedding picture, but then he's willing to do what I want instead of what he wants." She blew him a kiss and held the door open for Dixie.

"To think I thought he'd marry something as low class as you. It's almost too funny to think about now. Take a bath, lady. Pay the money for a decent hair cut and invest in some makeup. The possibilities are slim but miracles can happen. Of course not with someone like Boone, but there is probably someone out there for you," Anita snarled her nose at the smell of the hot dogs.

"Honey, I only take baths on Fridays and that's a long way off. Makeup is something I do when Boone and I fight, and I don't believe in miracles, but I'm trying. I've got an appointment with a tattoo specialist today to put a little angel on my fanny to help me believe," Dixie shot right back.

"You are so disgusting," Anita got in the last word and practically ran out of the shop.

"She came to propose to me one more time." Boone reached for the box with the hot dogs.

"I'm taking it you didn't accept." Dixie held her breath. Something would go wrong. Murphy's Law was written just for her.

"No, we want different things. Ah, onions. Come here, lady," he pulled her through the swinging gate and wrapped his arms around her, hugging her close and liking the way she fit against his chest. He tilted her head back and kissed her soundly, tasting cool root beer still lingering on her tongue.

"Onions cause that? Or do you like women who need a bath, a decent hairdo and some makeup?" she asked when he ended the kiss. She leaned against him another moment, not trusting her knees to support her.

"No, onions don't cause it. You do. And darlin', I happen to like you just the way you are. I can't see Anita helping clean up the mess this shop was in early this morning. And let me tell you something, that smudge of dirt right there on your chin is just plumb sexy. And the kiss is because after I devour all those onions, you won't want me near you," he said.

She skinnied out of his arms, laughing all the time. "You got a lot to learn, Mr. Daniel Boone Callahan. I like onions. Love them. I could kiss you all night after you've eaten onions and root beer."

"Anita . . ." he started and stopped.

"Didn't like onions," she finished for him. "Neither did Todd. We're special, honey. And special people belong together."

"I would say so. Now is that all you wanted to talk

about?" He bit into the hot dog. The cheese was melted perfectly, the chili still hot.

"No, I got a lot to say, but I want you to go first so I know exactly what it is you want out of life," she said.

"Fair enough. I want a home. Own one in San Antonio and twenty acres with it. Nothing real fancy. Three-bedroom brick with a big patio and a front porch complete with a couple of rocking chairs. But I want someone to share it with, Dixie. Someone who'll have my children and look after my heart. However, that scares the liver out of me and I mean it. At my age, which is thirty-six by the way, it's time for me to settle down and have a family. Way past due. And I'm wanting to do that. But I don't want to also. I want to come to Florida every year. I don't want to give up my freedom to do that, so I'd be asking a woman to live in an RV without a washer and dryer and a bathroom so tiny you couldn't cuss a cat in it without getting a hair in your mouth. I don't want to have to stay home because the kids are playing summer league ball or dancing in some ballet recital. I want to bring them to Florida and teach them to work in the T-shirt shop, live on the beach and show them a life without fancy things. But I want them to have all the other things just like I did when I was a kid. Am I making a bit of sense?" He picked up the root beer and drank long and deep.

"More than you'll ever know," she said.

"I'm glad you think so, because it just sends my senses reeling. It's like a never-ending puzzle," he told her.

"That's because you're from Mars," she teased. "Here, finish my hot dog. I'm full."

"Good lord have mercy upon my soul, this woman is finally full. The world will come to an end today," Boone laughed nervously. He'd just bared his soul to her and she hadn't told him he was stark raving mad. That had to be a good sign.

"Yes, she is and she's fixing to do a bit of oration, so clean off a spot and get ready," she told him. "To begin with, I want to teach. But I might not want to when I have children, which I do want, by the way. I want a whole houseful of them just like my parents had so there's bickering and loving everywhere. If I do want to continue to work though I want to be able to do it without some kind of fight with my husband. I just want to be treated like an equal, not a child or as Faith says, a trophy wife to attend formal functions and then leave my husband to hell alone while he does whatever he wants. I want to be a part of his life down to the decisions about whether to plant roses or cactus in the front yard flower bed. I want all those things but I want independence, too. Now does that make a bit of sense?" she asked.

"More than you'll ever know. What if this relationship goes all the way to the altar, Dixie? I'm not rushing things here. I'm just asking. What if it does? Would you move away from that big family?" he asked.

"That's rushing, Boone. Right now I'm content with a few good old onion kisses. I'm not ready for the altar scene just yet," she told him.

"Is it the Irish thing?" he asked.

"No, I haven't got a prejudiced cell in my body. Unless you count those where I detest men who are male chauvinist hogs," she said.

"Pigs. Male chauvinist pigs," he corrected her.

"No, Boone, a pig is just a baby. If a man is a male chauvinist, he's a full grown hog," she said.

"Then if it's not the Irish thing, then what?" he asked.

"We just got on the ship and we've got a lot of getting to know each other between here and the time I get off the ship at the end of the summer," she told him.

"There were arguments in the book," he said.

"Yes, and I expect there'll be some here, too," she told him.

"What happens if one day I really do fire you?"

"What happens if one day I really do quit?"

"Guess we'll cross that bridge when we get to it," he said.

"Or blow the sucker up," Dixie grinned.

The smile was irresistible. He leaned forward without touching her and kissed her onion and root beer mouth.

"Mmmm," she said. "Nice beginnings there, Captain Boone."

"I thought so," he said.

"Hey, hey, you two, stop kissing and listen to me." Faith came sweeping in the room. A tall blond, dressed in a bikini with a sarong wrapped up under her arms. "Jill says to tell you that Monday night is still on. Paul is going to California and she'll be flying out there on Tuesday. Jackson wants to know if you'd be game for a round or two of miniature golf tonight, Boone? He's taking a week off and tomorrow we're going to Canada to talk to someone up there about a game and play the rest of the week."

Boone nodded without even looking up at Faith. "Tell Jackson I'll be ready soon as I close shop at nine. What time does the Periwicks start?"

"Nine is good enough for all of us. I'll send him down here right before closing. And Dixie, you better not be late." Faith left in a flurry of swirling silk.

"Not for the world," Dixie told her.

"Or for Boone?" he asked quietly.

"This could be the most important part of our friendship, likeship, loveship . . . all ships, like the ship in the book. What goes on in the PMS Club is secret. It lets us vent with no hard feelings. Men need that too, but you're too stubborn to realize it," she said.

"Are we fighting?" he asked.

"Maybe, but a kiss might be the start of making up," she told him, rolling up onto her tiptoes and wrapping her arms around his neck.

"I've got a feeling this ship is ready to sail," he whispered in her ear.

"Then anchors away, Captain Boone," she said.

Chapter Fourteen

Jill fastened her periapt around her neck, checking her reflection in the stainless steel refrigerator door. She packed six bologna and cheese sandwiches in a wicker hamper. Tucked in a bag of potato chips and a jar of dill pickles. She picked up six sodas from the refrigerator by the plastic ring that held all of them together. She was ready.

Faith fastened her periapt, checking her reflection in the glass patio door. She kicked off her sandals, retied the sarong around her waist and pulled her blond locks back into a ponytail at the nape of her neck. She grabbed the blanket from the back of the sofa and three worn pillows. She was ready.

Dixie fastened her periapt and tugged on the filigreed silver to make sure the hook would hold. Pulling three still warm towels from the dryer, she buried her face in them, inhaling deeply. They smelled like Florida. Like freedom. Like love. She was ready.

They trooped out the back door in single file without saying a word. Down the stairs; Jill first, then Faith, and Dixie bringing up the rear. When they reached the empty beach, Faith fluffed out the blanket. Jill set the food basket and sodas in the middle of it. Dixie tossed the towels off to one side.

"Who's hungry?" Jill asked.

"All of us," Faith said. "At this moment I officially call this order of the PMS Club to its last meeting in Florida. Hand me a bologna sandwich and a root beer. So who goes first? Has it been a good summer?"

Dixie took her first sandwich from Jill's hand and nodded. "Wonderful summer, but I'm ready to go home. Every year at the end of the school term I think I'd rather dig ditches or perfect my 'Would you like that supersized?' speech. But when summer is over, even an exciting one like this, I'm ready for the classroom."

"But has the excitement of this summer sent us all running to the classroom because it's our escape hatch?" Jill asked.

"Probably." Dixie nodded seriously.

"Okay, I'm going first before we get into philoso-phizin' so deep we forget to talk about the men folks," Faith said.

"Okay, what did you and Jackson decide. Are you in a hurry to get this meeting over so you can go spend a few more precious hours with him?" Dixie asked.

Faith took a long breath and let it out slowly. "He left on a two o'clock flight to Marion, Virginia, for a couple of weeks. Family reunion time. He invited me to go with him, but I told him we should spend some time apart to see if our relationship is real or just the product of an incredible summer. We're going to see each other at Thanksgiving. I'm going home to New Orleans for the first time since I left. We're doing the family thing with Mother's kin folks. The whole round of social parties. Big meals. All of it. I've asked Jackson to go with me and meet them."

"You're surely not going three months without seeing him?" Jill said.

"Of course not, silly woman," Faith laughed. "Two weeks. That's long enough to see if it's an out of sight, out of mind thing. I'll be making lots of trips to Little Rock to pick him up at the airport, and making a few weekend trips of my own between now and then."

"Do you love him? Really love him or has this just been like you said, an incredible summer?" Jill asked.

"I love him, but there's nine years between us. I want to be sure before we go doing anything stupid like buying two left-hand rings and flying to Las Vegas or Cancun," Faith said.

"But you told me if you ever married I could be a brides maid and wear a pink dress with a big fancy hat," Dixie teased.

"You can. It'd be a little hot in Cancun on the beach but if you want to wear pink taffeta and a southern belle hat with white lace, you can sure do it," Faith said.

"When do you think this might take place?" Dixie asked.

"I'm not in a hurry. Maybe next summer." Faith

grinned. "But don't say a word to Jackson. It's going to be his idea. Now your turn, Jill. What's going on with Paul? You've been keeping steady company with him. Flying off here, there and yonder. Teaching is going to be dull after all the rubbing elbows with the rich and shameless that you've been doing."

"Yes, it is," Jill said. "But we need some time apart, too. You were right about one thing, Faith. He's the smothering type. Not that I don't like all the attention, but I need just a little bit of breathing space to see if it's all real. Right now I feel like I've been the princess in a fairy tale and I'm going to wake up to find it's a dream," she said.

"Sugar, those are not glass slippers on your feet. It's been real, all right," Faith said. "And Travis, I mean Paul, can change, too. Make him compromise a little. Even if you decide to buy those left-handed gold bands and say the vows with him, don't let him smother your identity away. Remember he fell in love with you as you are and he wouldn't love you if you weren't that woman."

"So when are you seeing him again? Didn't you two say your good-byes last night?" Dixie asked.

"Yes, we did. He asked me if he should sing 'The Rose' again and bring roses," Jill smiled. "I told him it wouldn't have the same effect if it wasn't raining. He'll be flying into the little Conway airport in a couple of weeks when he finishes a deal he's working on in California. We're working toward the idea . . ." Jill paused.

"You're engaged!" Faith all but shouted.

"Not really. Just unofficially. He asked me and I said

yes, but not until we've had some cool-off time. Some time when I'm back at the job, when we aren't seeing each other for several days out of every single week. When things are mundane and normal. Everyone looks like an angel when you're floating in the clouds. I just want to be sure," she said.

"Did he have a ring ready?" Dixie asked.

"No, we're going to pick one out and announce it in October if it's all still working by then," Jill said.

"When's the wedding?" Faith asked.

"He'd like a Thanksgiving one. I'm thinking Christmas with red velvet for both of you. In Tulsa with all our friends and family," Jill said.

"No hats?" Dixie teased.

"You think I'd have a wedding with no hats? I'm marrying one of the richest men in all Louisiana and all his relatives will be there with the smell of money oozing out their pores. Yes, we're going to wear hats. Santa Claus hats. And you two are going to wear those little red velvet dresses that come up to your hineys with white fur trim around the bottom. I was thinking about you both wearing necklaces of jingle bells. After the wedding Paul and I would ride off to the honeymoon in a sleigh pulled by reindeer. Surely Paul can find me reindeer if I have my heart set on them," Jill said.

For a few minutes it sounded like a whole gaggle of third grade girls had just found a peephole in the boy's bathroom.

"I'll personally fund the whole wedding if you'll do that," Faith wiped tears from her cheeks. "It would be worth every cent to see Travis Paul Beauchamp's face when Dixie and I strolled down the aisle. Could we carry fake red poinsettias in our bouquets, all tied with bright gold ribbons? And maybe your veil can be held in a halo of cedar with bright red Christmas tree ornaments hot glued to it. You'd better pass out smelling salts rather than rice or birdseed in those little beribboned pouches."

"These periapts aren't working," Dixie said. "We're still in more mischief than we found all year in Arkansas."

"Mumbo jumbo, hickory dickory dock," Faith intoned dramatically, looking up at the moon. She moved her hands in circles around all three of them. She picked up sand and flung it over her left shoulder and drank half a can of root beer, bringing forth a loud burp at the end. "That should take care of it," she declared.

"Oh, that's been the whole problem, all along," Dixie said. "You forgot to burp."

"I told you before. I only know part of the voodoo. I had to listen at the window when Aunt Gertrude went to the Marie Laveau sessions. There was this chanting and then there was some quietness and I'd forgotten the burp," Faith said.

"Are you sure it was a soda burp? Maybe they were strangling a bullfrog?" Dixie said.

"Or maybe they'd just eaten too much Cajun rice and beans," Jill said.

"All about the same noise so the voodoo queens might not know the difference," Faith said.

"Okay, we are duly protected," Jill said. "Now what about Boone, Dixie?"

"His RV's headed toward the setting sun this afternoon. Like the cowboy riding off into the sunset in the old westerns," Dixie said.

"When are you seeing him again?" Faith asked.

"Fall break. He won't be flying in and out. We'll be the poor country cousins you two feel sorry for and come to visit. But we'll try to keep you fed and happy while you are there," Dixie said.

"So that means there is a *we* in the future?" Jill asked.

"Yes, I think it does. Not tomorrow future, but maybe a Christmas future like you talked about, Jill. We're going to be patient and see. He's coming to Arkansas for fall break and to meet my folks. We'll see how things go then. If the fire is still hot or if the embers have cooled," Dixie said.

"Sugar, the way that man looks at you, it would take more than eight weeks to make the embers go cold," Faith said.

"I hope so. I really do. The physical chemistry is there and I love him. I want to be sure, though. Sure that it's my heart and not my biological clock," Dixie said.

"I can see it now." Faith used the picnic basket like an imaginary crystal ball, moving her hands in slow circles over the top of it. "We'll have our PMS meetings on Monday nights in San Antonio at Dixie's place. Mr. Beauchamp has his own plane so he can damn well keep it free on that night for the pilot to take Jill to the meeting. After all, there's nothing more important than that. And I'm rich as Midas but Jackson is richer so I'll just use the commercial lines once a week. Dixie can pick us up at the airport and we'll have our Periapt Magnolia Sisterhood meetings on schedule."

"Do you think we'll stay that close?" Jill asked.

"Yes, ma'am," Faith said. "We have to. We owe it to the Sisterhood."

"Ahem," a deep, masculine voice said from the bottom of the stairs. "What are you doing out here this late? The sun has already set."

"Todd?" Dixie said. "Is that you?"

"Of course it's me. What other man would be coming around this late at night?" Todd started toward them. "I'd like to talk to Dixie in private, please."

"What other man?" Faith whispered with a low giggle.

"Whatever you have to say, you can say it in front of Jill and Faith," Dixie said without moving from her spot on the blanket.

"The summer is over and I've come to take you home. I thought we'd stop in Memphis and get married tomorrow afternoon. I told the principal to expect a phone call by five tomorrow that you'd be quitting your job." Todd folded his arms across his chest and looked down on the three women. "I've been a patient man, Dixie. I've let you have a final fling with your friends, and now it's time to grow up."

"Well, Todd Riley, I do thank you for all your patience and generosity. But the answer is no. I'm not interested in being your wife and I'll call my principal first thing in the morning and tell him you were wrong," Dixie told him.

"You are making a big mistake. Everyone in Arkansas will think you're insane to turn me down.

Want to curb that hot temper of yours and think about it a minute?" he asked.

Dixie gathered up the three towels they hadn't even used since they hadn't gone for a final midnight swim. Faith followed suit, shaking the dust from the blanket and making sure she had all three pillows. Jill tucked the last can of root beer and all the trash into the picnic basket.

"Well?" Todd asked.

"No, I don't want to think about it. I don't love you, Todd. I'm sorry you made the trip to Florida in vain," Dixie said.

"Oh, I didn't just come to see you. I had some business over in Destin," he said.

"I'm glad," Dixie said. "Hope it went well for you or goes well if you haven't been there yet. And, Todd, next time you propose to a woman, remember how you did it the first time. You must have had a little more finesse then or your wife would have sent you packing."

"There's a whole string of women out there who'd be glad to marry me," he all but growled.

"Then by all means, go pick one from the lot of them and I wish you the best," Dixie said.

The three of them left him shaking sand from the cuffs of his Armani slacks.

"So what's the difference, other than money?" Faith asked when they were back at the house and they'd heard Todd's rental car peel out of the driveway.

"Between Todd and Boone?" Dixie asked.

Faith nodded.

"I feel sorry for Todd tonight. Really, I do. I'm not

even mad at him and I hope he finds someone to make him happy," Dixie said.

"That didn't answer the question. They both offer you marriage. Todd is so rich you'd be able to meet us for PMS meetings in Paris or London. Both want the same things. A family. Kids. The house with a yard," Jill said.

"Todd demands it with no consideration to what I want and what makes me happy. Boone and I discuss everything," Dixie tried to explain. "Besides, I just plain fell in love with Boone and I only thought I loved Todd. It's like the difference in doing the laundry out on the back porch using a rub board and galvanized washtub, or doing it in the house with a fully automatic brand-new Maytag."

"Good enough," Faith said. "So I'm taking all the wonderful memories of Jackson, plus the hope of a bright future home with me. Is that acceptable? We have to agree on the one thing we're taking home, remember?"

"Agreeable with me," Dixie said.

"And me," Jill nodded.

"I'm taking home memories and what I hope turns out to be a lifetime of memories." Jill uncorked a bottle of cheap wine and poured up three glasses. "Is that all right with both of you? Especially you, Faith?"

"I can live with it right well." Faith picked up a glass of wine.

"Me, too," Dixie did the same. "I'm taking home a biological clock that has been smashed. It doesn't need a battery anymore, because I've figured out that any man doesn't beat no man at all. I'm taking Boone home. Memories, hopes, love, the whole nine yards and praying that reality and fantasy can live happily ever after like in the romance books."

"We'll let you take that home," Jill said and Faith nodded.

They clinked their glasses together.

"This meeting of the PMS Club is adjourned until next Monday night at Jill's house. Tomorrow morning we go home and see if the fairy tale can endure real life," Faith said.

"Mumbo jumbo, hickory dickory dock," Jill and Dixie said in unison.

Made in the USA
Monee, IL
29 April 2023